Summer in Ville-Marie

Summer

Paule Daveluy

in Ville-Marie

translated from the French by Monroe Stearns

Holt, Rinehart and Winston   *New York*

Library of Congress Catalog Card Number: 62-11173

91736-0112
Printed in the United States of America

To my daughters—

Danielle, Sylviane, Brigitte, Marie-Claude

"This book is a novel; its characters are mere inventions. Whoever thinks that in them he recognizes real human beings, living or dead, demonstrates that he does not know what a novel is or what characters are."

—André Maurois

Summer in Ville-Marie

Chapter 1

AREN'T WE EVER going to get there?"

Rosanne could not bear it any longer. From one year to the next, she used to wait for that magic moment, the prelude to vacation, when she and her Vadeboncoeur relatives drove up to the village of Ville-Marie. She was like a cat, waiting to spring on a mouse the second it darts out of its hole. Intensely, she yearned for the instant of arrival, the way everyone, no matter what her age longs for a promised happiness.

The summer of her sixteenth year was beginning, and she was ready for it: shapely, tall, her skin smooth as cream, her eyes two dancing tawny lights under unruly brown hair, her disposition that of still waters running deep.

Just the same, the swaying of the automobile and the long trip had subdued her excitement. She leaned her head, heavy with fatigue, on her cousin Colette's shoulder, jammed her feet between two cartons, and twisted her body every which way.

All six of them—Uncle Henri, and Aunt Adèle; Rosanne's cousins, Colette, Marilou, and Henriette; and Rosanne herself—were very tired and cramped in the gray Packard. They had driven five hundred miles over rough roads from Montréal, Rosanne's home, on their way to Ville-Marie on lake Témiscamingue, where the Vadeboncoeurs lived.

"Poems of dust, these roads," Uncle Henri kept saying. He was so right. The roads had a positive genius for avoiding anything like a straight line as they meandered through the Canadian woods. Driving on them was nerve-wracking because they zigzagged up even the smallest hills. At times, the travelers could see the landscape from three different angles at once.

"Papa," shouted Colette, the youngest, always wide awake, "according to the arrow, you should have turned left."

"Arrow? What arrow?" Uncle Henri grumbled, startled out of his reverie.

Aunt Adèle, in a hurry to get home, shrugged. "The arrow of the Last of the Mohicans, stupid!" she said.

They backed up to the signpost in a cloud of dust, only to find that no one could figure out in which direction the arrow was pointing.

The signs had to be read from right to left, and one out of every three was missing. Then there were the soft shoulders of the road, or the deep ditches, and the railroad crossings at which Uncle Henri, who was the soul of caution, would stop and listen and scan the horizon on both sides.

No billboards shut out the view of the fields, so it was easy for the girls to keep up their game of wetting their thumbs and stamping them on their palms, counting the white horses that would carry them to their dream men. One hundred horses, and the next man one saw would be he.

"Ninety-nine, one hundred!" gay, plump Marilou shouted triumphantly. "Now where's my Prince Charming?"

To their amusement, it happened that the next man they saw was a ragged old tramp, completely astonished at the kisses they blew him as they drove past. Their laughter echoed along the road.

Uncle Henri was no speed demon, and when a car going forty miles an hour passed them, he hollered, "Go on, go on, that's the way to kill yourself!" Aunt Adèle tried to quiet him down by agreeing, "That's the right way to drive. Right into the ditch!"

The car bumped slowly over the road leading through the woods, which seemed to swallow it up hungrily. The road grew even more winding. Rosanne found the dark green underbush full of enchantment, and every little logging trail tempted her to follow it to some mysterious cavern. Looking upward, she would gaze at the lacy patterns of the leaves against the sky, or search among the dark brown tree trunks for the gleam of a slender white birch. Uncle Henri knew the names of all the trees, and he ticked them off as they drove by, partly to increase the girls' meager store of knowledge, partly to show off his own.

Deep in the woods, they traveled past calm lakes with irregular shores, their glassy surfaces reflecting the somber green of the forest, as pure and refreshing as a glass of cold water on a hot day.

Almost always the lakes were deserted, except for the white water lilies that ringed their edges and the dragonflies hovering on iridescent wings among the reeds. But their loneliness was not oppressive; rather it possessed a certain primitive purity, haunted by the melancholy cries of the ospreys. The trees hemmed the car so closely that Rosanne could reach out and pick branches of leaves for fly swatters.

"This scenery bores me to death," complained Marilou, pouting like a child in spite of the fact that she would be eighteen the next winter. "It's like a graveyard. I want to see some more people."

She soon got her wish, for the car came to a gang of young roadworkers, stripped to the waist and streaming with sweat. They moved agilely out of the way, waving and blowing kisses.

"Hey, sweethearts!" they shouted, their hands framing their mouths. "Slow up and give us a kiss!"

Uncle Henri was a little scared of them and scowled fiercely.

"Come on there, Grandpa," they kept on, "you've got more than enough for yourself. Lend us one or two; we ain't going to eat them!"

At last they crossed the hundred barren and starkly desolate miles of the Timagami Reservation. Now behind them was Cobalt, the town that had lived briefly and extravagantly, exhausting both the mines and the miners, and then died. Then—after Tête-du-Lac, with its crude bridge over the Quinze Rapids of the Outaouais River, the natural boundary between Quebec and Ontario; after the sleepy village of Guigues and the final endless miles—they reached their destination.

Halfway up the hill that hid the village, Aunt Adèle said to her excited niece and daughters, "We're almost there. Get ready!"

Uncle Henri teased them by pretending to be very apprehensive. "You'll see. Ville-Marie will have burned up while we were away. Those forest fires don't stop at anything short of a tidal wave. It will have all gone up in smoke."

"Come on, Papa," exclaimed Henriette, who usually believed everything her father said, "how can there be a tidal wave in a lake?"

"Our lake is no ordinary one, my pet. Témiscamingue is seventy-five miles long. It's a real inland sea."

Then he put the car in low gear so that it crawled along like a stubborn horse, driving the girls crazy with impatience.

Aunt Adèle enjoyed the joke as much as he. She shared her daughters' joy at returning to the village after nine dreary months in boarding school, but it was Rosanne she watched out of the corner of her eye, as if she could not understand her niece's feverish delight. Every year, as the car approached the summit of the hill, Rosanne's enthusiasm was the same.

It was always a fine day when they returned, and Rosanne could never discover how her uncle could be such a good weather prophet. In fact, she used to think him a sort of magician, for when they left Ville-Marie, it was always foggy and rainy, making their farewells even sadder.

Rosanne clutched the window frame and leaned out of the car, staring wide-eyed and breathing deeply. "Smell the wild strawberries!" She tugged Colette, her summer-sister, toward her so that she, too, might whiff the fragrance.

The young faces blocking the window looked very much alike—offspring of the same stock, with upturned noses and wind-swept hair—Colette darker of eyes and curls, fairer of skin, secure in a newly acquired sophistication; Rosanne more slender, in a way more beautiful, but still gauche in behavior, gawky and shy as a newborn lamb.

"That's not strawberries," Uncle Henri said. "It's sweet clover."

"Strawberries!" Rosanne was adamant.

"Sweet clover!"

Neither one would give in.

Beside the car the rich fields of the farming region reached as far as the eye could see, the dusty road snaking between them. The oats were already ripe, and in the irrigation ditches the scarlet of the wild strawberries stained the dark green carpet of moss.

"Please hurry, Papa!" urged Marilou.

Finally the heavy car reached the top of the hill and stopped. Rosanne could not contain herself a moment longer.

"We're here! We're here!" she shouted. "It's Ville-Marie at last! Oh, Aunt Adèle, isn't it beautiful!"

The village lay before them, warming itself like a lizard

in the June sun. The ring of hills ended at the docks where the lake curved into a bay. The houses of the village were scattered on the lower slopes; to the left the church spire rose out of the treetops. The convent, the high school, the barn of the farmers' co-operative, and the courthouse, set back from the water, overlooked the houses. A cemetery, with flowers growing in neat patches beside the gravestones, lay on the crest of the nearest hill. Close to it was a grotto—copied from the one at Lourdes—to which the inhabitants of the region often made pilgrimages.

Rosanne would have liked to take the whole scene in her arms and hug it to her. This was her Ville-Marie, the golden, the meek, surely the loveliest place on earth. Ville-Marie, deeply rooted in the Quebec soil with its Roman Catholic soul and French-Canadian ways.

Colette was laughing both out of her own delight and at Rosanne's. The two were to share not only this moment but many others, whether pleasurable or sad, that the summer held in store.

Uncle Henri stepped on the accelerator and they sped down the hill.

"Now you will see, my little tigresses," he said, rolling the "r" of his native Quebec accent until he seemed to be roaring. "We are going to enter the village in style."

They shot down the last grade in such a cloud of dust that no one could have recognized either the car or its passengers. The horn was blasting away as they drove along Convent Street. There was no one on the sidewalk, no one at the windows. Yet, ten minutes later, everyone in town knew that the Vadeboncoeur sisters were back from boarding school and that their cousin, Rosanne Fontaine, was with them.

They stopped at Grandmamma Guay's house, Castel Riant, to tell her they had arrived. It was as if to say the life of the village could resume now the Vadeboncoeurs were there. Aunt Adèle's sisters (Estelle and Reine) and their husbands (Uncle Alphonse and Uncle Sylvio) had gathered there as they did on every occasion of importance to the family.

The aunts kissed Rosanne, inquiring about the weather in Montréal, asking about her young brothers and her mother, poor widowed Laurence, so unlucky yet so brave. The girl gave two kisses in return for each one she got. Everyone was chattering like a flock of parakeets. What a close, warm, happy family was hers, Rosanne thought. Each of her mother's sisters seemed to embody the entire magic of the village, as if, like good fairies, they were bestowing their gifts on the impoverished niece, restored to them each summer.

The voyagers' last stop was at the home of Narcisse Bérubé, caretaker, it seemed, for all of Ville-Marie. He kept the key to the Vadeboncoeur house, cared for Colette's cat and dog, and for Aunt Adèle's potted plants.

Nothing had burned up, or blown away, or changed. In the gentle shade of its giant elms their house awaited their attack upon it from behind its willow hedge, the sunlight streaming through the leafy branches onto the clematis that swarmed over the porch.

"Well, let's go," Uncle Henri said a little impatiently. "End of the line! Everybody out!"

Now came the struggles with the heaps of baggage— umbrellas, rubbers, raincoats, oilskins, heavy overcoats, light overcoats—for he always took every precaution against changes in the weather. When the trunk of the car was full, the rest was piled helter-skelter inside, the clothes Rosanne's cousins had brought from boarding school, her own things stuffed into a cardboard suitcase, and the tokens of Aunt Adèle's shopping spree in Montréal.

Just as every other year, Colette and Rosanne had to be caught by the hems of their skirts and tugged back to the house, crestfallen at not being able to escape to the fields to see who could find the first wild strawberry.

Chapter 2

THE VADEBONCOEUR HOUSE was an inviting and friendly one. Aunt Adèle, however, thought it too cramped; and every summer, Uncle Henri planned to knock down some partitions or add a wing, but wisely ended by letting well enough alone. Rosanne loved the place just as it was, warm and vibrant as a living thing.

One got used to the soapbox shape and the gingerbread trim that culminated in a pointed roof, and even admired the clematis-covered pillars along the front that supported the balcony and framed the porch. Everything about the house—the freshly painted clapboards, the hanging flower baskets on the porch, the quaint cupola, and even the copper plate by the front door that identified it as the residence of *Charles-Henri Vadeboncoeur, Surveyor*—said, "Welcome! Please come in."

The rooms contained a conglomeration of vastly differing styles of furniture, all comfortable and all arranged with small regard for elegance. Inside, near the front door, was the barometer, which ruled every moment of the family's day. The first thing Uncle Henri did in the morning was to consult this handsome mahogany instrument, which was the envy of his brothers-in-law. The needle used to wobble when one tapped the case to make the weather prediction more favorable. In Montréal, even the hot dog days of July and August were of no concern to Rosanne; but here she had to know exactly what the weather would be like. On the barometer's word hung every picnic, every tennis match, every excursion to the nearby villages of Laverlochère or Fugèreville in search of a maid for Aunt Adèle or a cook for Uncle Henri's land-surveying trips.

The front hall was the size of a handkerchief. "What a pity it is!" Aunt Adèle used to complain, for she could never get accustomed to this tiny vestibule after the enormous foyer of her father's house.

As soon as one crossed the threshold, there was the steep staircase, padded with thick carpeting. The left wall was studded with clothes-hooks.

"Hideous!" Aunt Adèle would groan, for she hated having the family's wearing apparel exposed to view.

"Adèle," her husband would growl severely, "you will get rid of those hooks over my dead body."

"But you promised you would hang only your coat and hat there, and now look at that mess."

He would look at the assortment of articles adorning

the hooks, shrug, smile a little foolishly, but never yield an inch of ground. Ten minutes later all the cousins' clothes would be mysteriously stowed away in the kitchen closet, and nothing would be left on the hooks but the two permitted items, coat and hat. Under his gentle exterior Uncle Henri was a firm disciplinarian.

The other wall of the staircase was made of latticed wood, hung with a flower-patterned Oriental rug. All the woodwork was painted white, making the rug seem even more colorful, and white bookcases formed a passageway to the parlor.

Aunt Adèle herself had decorated the parlor while Uncle Henri was away on one of his long business trips. She had brought down from the attic a wicker sofa and two old-fashioned chairs, which she had painted yellow and upholstered in flowered chintz. The room was like a sunny garden, for big windows let in plenty of light, and there were pots of ivy and ferns on the sills.

Aunt Adèle had a green thumb, and she was also good at making things with her hands, such as startlingly realistic ornamental plaques molded out of papier-mâché and painted with the bright colors she loved, or needlepoint that seemed to live and breathe in the sunlight.

This room was, indeed, the very heart of the house. There, Uncle Henri elected to spend much of his time in a brass-studded armchair, hunched close to the radio which he forever fiddled with, trying to get short-wave broadcasts from England, France, or Germany, while he stroked the cat with his free hand.

In contrast to the parlor's charm, the adjoining living room, with its velvet draperies, horsehair furniture and the upright piano heaped high with scores, was stuffy and dark. But everyone in the household had a special love for that piano. Uncle Henri would play the sentimental waltz he had composed twenty years earlier, which he called "The Adèle Waltz," while Aunt Adèle sat on the bench beside him, striking notes at random. Henriette worked hard at Chopin's "Polonaise." When her father's eye was on her, Marilou would stick to scales and exercises, but as soon as he left the room, she would swing into jazz. When he made her return to a more classical repertory, she would play Ravel's "Boléro," on which she had spent hours of practice in an attempt to work up to its fastest rhythms. She never seemed to tire of it, and eventually she could play it fairly well or, at least, fairly loudly.

Colette and Rosanne would run from the living room as soon as they heard her strike the first notes, and she returned the compliment when the two of them crossed hands in their duets. The left-hand part, the easier, was given to Rosanne, since she could not manage the trickier right hand and still keep in time. The house reverberated when they settled on *Alouette, gentille Alouette,* which Colette used to embellish with masterful inventions.

Aunt Adèle covered her ears with her hands, but she seldom stopped them, for she was the soul of patience. There couldn't have been a better aunt for making a summer vacation a success, Rosanne felt. She was cheerful, easygoing, and sympathetic.

Rosanne liked to feel she was the perfect poor-relation guest, for she was as docile as a mollusk, well brought up, and healthy. In the evenings, if she was not at the piano, she would be lost in a book, riffling the corner of every page in her intense concentration, for she was crazy about reading. But she used to eat enough for ten, and she was often in the kitchen, nibbling or sniffing at something. The kitchen was a cheerful, blue and white room, scrubbed until it shone. On one side were three doors in a row: to the wine cellar, to the catch-all closet where the garments ripped from the hooks in the hall were dumped, to the pantry where rows and rows of mouth-watering table delicacies tempted the appetite. Uncle Henri bought foodstuffs wholesale, to feed his working parties when they went into the woods to survey.

The slope-roofed shed, added to the house as an after-thought, contained the washtubs and other laundering equipment. It belonged to Youki, Colette's spaniel, and to her cat, Tempest, a white ball of fur Colette had rescued two summers before, when some neighbors were going to drown it in their rain barrel. Aunt Adèle had no love for cats, but Colette pleaded so hard to keep the little animal that it was baptized Tempest in a Teapot. Youki and Tempest got on as well together as Colette and Rosanne did. At the end of the summer, when the cat proudly displayed four or five replicas of herself, the dog showed off as if he were their father.

Now the animals were running through the house, investigating every new scent. Youki would stop to lick someone's hand, Tempest would rub against Colette's leg and they would be off again. They semed to be as excited to be back in the house as Colette and Rosanne were.

Those two could not stop long enough to finish one job but dashed up and down stairs, unpacking summer clothes and tennis rackets with Marilou and Henriette; helping Uncle Henri open the windows to the fresh June air; or eating sweet bread, smeared with fresh butter, while Aunt Adèle was trying to prepare supper in the kitchen. They were back and the whole summer was before them.

Chapter 3

"ALL ABOARD FOR Lake Street and Grandmamma's house," said Uncle Henri as he got up from the table that evening after supper. "Wash your faces and come out to the car."

"Oh, no!" Marilou exclaimed. "I want to look up my old friends."

"You can see them tomorrow. Your grandmother is waiting for us."

Colette and Rosanne decided that they could not bear to ride in the car any more that day, so they began to saunter, arm in arm, toward the village. The rest of the family followed them slowly, Uncle Henri bringing up the rear, grumpy at having to walk but secretly delighting in the quiet dusk and the shadowy trees overhanging the road. Rosanne never tired of tramping over the wooden sidewalks of the village. As she stepped on them, each plank gave off a different sound, and she and Colette were soon trying to see who could make the boards thump the loudest. Grass grew right up to the edge of the boards, and they pulled it up by the handful and nibbled the ends, sucking the tart juice.

Presently all six of them were at Aunt Reine's and Grandmamma's again to gossip and exchange family news.

Rosanne failed to notice how much more careworn was the dear lined face of her grandmother. Instead her eyes were busy peering into every nook and cranny of the living room, even behind the long velvet draperies and the potted plants, and then into the hall and the dining room, searching for one face—that of the young doctor of Ville-Marie, about whom she had been daydreaming since she first heard his name, Yves Renaud.

Over the winter Aunt Reine and Grandmamma had written eloquently about him in their letters to Rosanne's mother. Yves Renaud, they said, was dedicated to his work, handsome in a subdued way, quiet, well-mannered, clean to a fault, endowed with a wide intelligent forehead, a nose as straight as a carpenter's level and dark eyes whose mysterious sadness you could not help but want to console.

Colette had met the doctor the year before and promptly fallen in love with him. Rosanne had spent that summer with another aunt, who lived on Calumet Island in the Barry River. Colette had never breathed a word of her feelings, and she had not written to Rosanne. Their friendship, which was so intense in July and August, when they were together in Ville-Marie, lay dormant the rest of the year.

But it was easy for Rosanne to guess how Colette might have felt at the first smile she got from the handsome doctor. Eligible bachelors were a rarity in the village, and Colette and Rosanne had both spent many entrancing hours reading love stories without ever having anyone to fall in love with.

Yves Renaud, who was a sophisticated twenty-six, delighted the young girls of the village. They fought over him shamelessly. To Colette he looked so much like a hero of the Crusades that she could almost hear victorious trumpets when he drove by in his black Ford sedan.

Grandmamma's letters had hinted that Colette had fallen in love with Yves the minute he had set up practice in the office in the drugstore on the village square. Ville-Marie had needed a physician, so Uncle Sylvio, the mayor, had invited his young cousin to take over the vacant practice. Uncle Sylvio owed his college education and his law degree to Yves Renaud's father. An uncle by marriage, he had given the orphaned and ambitious young Sylvio both financial aid and affection.

For a generous man like Uncle Sylvio, who thought more of others' needs than of his own, gratitude was a sacred duty, and he felt keenly obliged to assist the son of his benefactor. He brought his protégé into the big house on Lake Street, and he and Aunt Reine, who had no children of their own, treated him as a son.

In Montréal Rosanne had read avidly the letters to her mother and had fashioned a highly desirable picture of the young doctor. She could scarcely wait for the next summer in Ville-Marie, and desperately hoped that Yves would find her attractive.

Now her searching eyes met her cousin's. With a flash of insight Rosanne realized that Colette was aware of her feelings. They were rivals. Her glance pleaded, "Don't be cross with me, Colette." Yet she resented Colette for just being there and for anticipating the pleasure of being the first to greet him; and she was sick at heart with the knowledge that her cousin felt the same way toward her.

Rosanne lost interest in the talk around her and concentrated on her own thoughts. Suddenly she heard Yves' name mentioned, and at once she was all attention.

"How is the doctor?" Aunt Adèle was asking with a touch of insincerity in her voice. She did not think so much of him since he had neglected her daughter. The summer before, he had been with Colette constantly, but after she went back to school in the fall, he seldom mentioned her name.

"Very well, indeed!" answered Aunt Reine, who had been waiting for a chance to get onto her favorite topic. "My dear, he works like a Trojan! They send for him from everywhere—Guigues, Lorrainville, even Fabre. He's out on his third call of the night right now."

Aunt Reine was pleased with the success of her protégé. She had been disturbed by the distrust Yves had encountered when he first arrived. Since he had cut short his internship to settle down in Ville-Marie, many villagers had doubted his competence, and patients had been slow in coming. Every time his name was mentioned, the rumors grew. In Ville-Marie rumors traveled quickly and everyone took a great interest in local gossip. When telephoning, it was necessary to talk in riddles to confuse the listeners on the party line. One wrapped an extra piece of paper around every letter before sealing it in an envelope. Let one indiscreet word drop, and peace and privacy were gone.

Some good soul would whisper, "What do you make of the new doctor?" and another would reply, "Well, he really seems a little wet behind the ears. He's had no surgical experience whatever, and as for what he knows about obstetrics, let's just not talk about that."

The villagers gave him a wide berth as long as they could, but eventually necessity won out. They had to call upon him to treat their boils and their measles and their pregnancies. Then they began to sing his praises.

"What a diagnostician he is!" Or "He can work wonders. Why, I'd trust him with anything. He really is even better than old Doctor Massicotte."

He treated those who could not pay, as well as those who could, and his devotion to his patients knew no limit. He would come at their first twinges of pain, at any hour of the day or night, even rowing across the lake in a storm to answer a call from one of the islands, or setting out in a snowplow-tractor over the impassable winter roads.

Rosanne delighted in hearing Aunt Reine and the others praise him.

Suddenly the conversation died on everyone's lips, and Rosanne was sure she felt her heart stop beating. The doctor had come into the room. He paused under the chandelier to smile at her grandmother, then to shake Uncle Henri's hand, and nod to everyone else. "Will he never be finished?" thought Rosanne, numb with anticipation. "Oh, how handsome he looks!" But what a pity he was not as tall or as athletic-looking as she had hoped. Just the same, she could not take her eyes off his dark, sensitive face.

Finally he came toward her, and she was introduced to him as ceremoniously as if she were being presented at court.

"Rosanne, this is Doctor Renaud . . . Doctor, this is our little Rosanne."

Her cheeks began to smolder as she felt him gazing at her. All she could manage to squeak out was a banal "How do you do, Doctor?" She could not help asking herself afterward what would have happened had she burst out with all she wanted to say, all that she had dreamed of saying at this first romantic meeting. She could imagine her relatives' jaws dropping, their hands flying to their mouths as they thought: "Poor Rosanne, she must be out of her mind!" And how would he have reacted? she wondered. Would he have taken her into his arms and kissed her as if to say, *"Ma chère,* I've been waiting for you, too." Someday, perhaps, she thought confidently, she would ask him.

Rosanne remained quietly seated beside her grandmother, scarcely daring to look up, yet wanting nothing more than to be able to stare unabashedly. The Vadeboncoeurs had left the house too quickly for her to put on the dress she had been keeping for just this moment. In fact, she had forgotten all about it. To her horror, she realized she was wearing a red polka-dot skirt which was not in the least seductive, and had tied a bandanna over her wind-blown hair.

"Good heavens!" Aunt Adèle had exclaimed, as she had caught sight of her niece running out of the door with Colette, "you look like Aunt Jemima."

Then the family had laughed at her resemblance to the familiar figure on the pancake-flour box.

Now, Rosanne squeezed her smarting eyes shut, waiting for the doctor to speak, quivering with expectation of his first words, intending to cherish them the rest of her life. But all he said was, "Ah!" No matter how many different intonations Rosanne gave that syllable, it still sounded cold and empty. She tried to find excuses for him. Perhaps he was afraid anything else he might say would be taken as having a deeper meaning, that Rosanne was just another of the many unmarried girls who would trap him with his own careless words if they could. Surely he must sense that she alone was different. Someone else might have been able to make more of that "Ah!", but not she. She could interpret it only as total indifference on his part, indifference to the importance of their first meeting.

But if he was miserly with words at the beginning, he was not stingy with his glances later. Aunt Adèle took that in, as she let Rosanne know when they got home by saying rather aggressively, "The doctor certainly could not take his eyes off you."

"Oh, do you really think so?" Rosanne said, as calmly

as if such attentions were a part of her daily life and all she had to do was crook her little finger to have every catch of the town on his knees to her. "I didn't notice," she added.

"You little liar," said her conscience. "You're really gloating. His eyes were so warm that you couldn't help but notice."

Colette was staring at Rosanne as if to reassure herself. "What do you think of him?" she asked, leaning over to catch the answer.

"Oh," Rosanne said, wrinkling her nose, "not much. He's just like anyone else." Then she added carelessly, "As a matter of fact, I like the athletic type better. They may not have much to say either, but they have more muscles."

Everyone burst out laughing at the doctor's expense. "Yves," murmured Rosanne to herself, "truly I thought you were as wonderful as any man could be. I don't care if you're not Mr. Universe."

Colette, obviously relieved, was smiling. "It's true. Yves is not very talkative, but that makes you pay all the more attention to what he does say."

"Yves must have learned suturing by practicing on his own mouth," Uncle Henri said, as innocent as a baby of the conflict he was harboring in his household.

"Now, don't you go and make him fall in love with you, Rosanne," warned Aunt Adèle, dutifully taking her daughter's side. "The doctor is flirtatious, and he likes to have girls trail after him, only to turn them off, pftt! as soon as they carry a torch for him."

"Not me," Rosanne said to herself. "I am different. I shall never let him out of my life."

Early the next afternoon, Rosanne met the doctor by chance. "Actually," she thought, "let's put it that I nudged fate a little, and let it go at that." She had seen to it that she was walking down the street alone when she was sure he would be going home to lunch.

She was coming out of the grocery store, her arms full of packages, when a car stopped behind her. Rosanne heard it and intuitively knew it was Yves. She felt sure that he must have arranged to catch up with her, too. All the same, she continued walking down the sidewalk, humming nonchalantly and keeping a tight rein on her curiosity. The motor raced, the black Ford rolled forward a little, and stopped again, right beside her.

"Mam'selle Rosanne," Yves said, looking at her reproachfully, "don't you greet your friends?"

Rosanne pretended surprise, and answered with a blush, "Oh, Doctor Renaud! I didn't recognize you."

"So there, my fine young man! So there, heart-smasher," she gloated. "If you think you can flirt with me, you'd better find out right away I'm no pushover." Yet, she knew that, so far as he was concerned, she would melt like gelatin in the sun.

"Well, now," he persisted, like a disappointed child, "don't you remember last evening at your grandmother's?"

"Oh, yes," she said without smiling, "you were the man in the gray suit who just said, 'Ah.' How do you do, Doctor?"

He looked her straight in the eye and laughed, as if he were pleased to find he had crossed swords with a worthy opponent. Rosanne smiled then. She knew her white sail-cloth skirt and her bright blue blouse were becoming. She was sure he had noticed her long bare legs, and she didn't mind that the sun was already beginning to freckle her nose.

"Won't you drive out to the fort with me?" he said, opening the car door. "I have to take some medicine to a patient."

"I suppose you need someone to hold the package?"

He laughed again, apparently delighted by her show of resistance.

"No, I want to get in your good graces. I must have seemed an awful fool to you last night."

"Has that 'Ah!' been bothering you?"

"Bothering me! I haven't been able to sleep on account of it."

"I should think you'd have prescribed a sleeping pill for yourself, if for no other reason than to test your own reme-dies."

"Don't be sarcastic, young lady. I wasn't very gracious, and I'm sorry. Somehow I always freeze up in groups of people."

"I suppose you're so used to getting your patients to say 'Ah!' that you think it's the proper way to start any con-versation?"

"You're terrible!"

"And you're very insensitive."

"But I was delighted to meet you. And to prove it, I'm asking you to go for a ride with me. Isn't that fair?"

"Fair enough."

Rosanne was having a hard time keeping up her pretenses, and she could feel a dimple coming into her cheek. The learned doctor was becoming human.

"So, get in, Rosanne."

"No, Doctor."

"I won't eat you, I promise. Please."

"I'm sorry . . ."

She really meant it. She had to refuse that first invitation in order to keep her independence, even though she was dying to be alone with him, to drive along roads whose banks were covered with June roses and honeysuckle, and revel in the pride of capturing the prey she had for so long planned to trap.

"I really can't," she said. "They're waiting for me at home."

"Well, that's my bad luck. Some other time, perhaps?"

"Some other time."

He drove off reluctantly. "Whenever you like," was what Rosanne really wanted to shout after his car. She sighed, half in satisfaction, half in regret. Then she began to look forward eagerly to "some other time."

At last her secret dream was about to come true—Yves would fall in love with her. But it meant that she would be competing with Colette, because it would not be possible to share Yves' attentions as they had shared Moïse Joly's two summers ago.

Chapter 4

COLETTE AND ROSANNE had passed that particular summer without a trace of rivalry or jealousy. They were never able to discover which of them Moïse Joly, a tall, good-looking farm boy, liked better, and it didn't matter. They had not the slightest intention of marrying him or anyone like him, and turning into farm wives to milk cows, kill flies, and plant cabbages. They knew perfectly well that, at fourteen, love is something that should happen time and time again, but still, they had dreamed of proving that they were no longer children.

None of the boys in the village had ever excited their affections. Uncle Henri's assistant, Jean-Claude, was refined, shy, well-dressed, and—engaged. So he belonged among the untouchables. Then there was Cousin Octave, Aunt Estelle's son. His lack of humor and his utterly proper manner made him their favorite laughingstock, and they used to tease him by chirping a popular saying of the day, "Octave is all we've got; poor stuff and not enough."

Even so, Rosanne and Colette found his persistent attentions rather touching. He would print the rolls of photographs they took with their Brownie camera, and not be bothered by their impatient demands that he hurry. They would go back to his darkroom every fifteen minutes to ask why he wasn't finished, for heaven's sake; and they would rip the sensitized paper off the wet film, trying to see which one could manage to upset his slow, methodical habits. Sometimes they would go too far with their teasing, and he would lose patience and shout, "You two are nothing but a couple of pests."

Colette would get down on her knees on the bottom step of the staircase and, with folded hands and lowered head, would piously murmur, "Saint Octave, patron of pests, pray for us." Then even Octave would have to laugh.

To give him his due, he was really a good sort for all his lack of personality, which, in a sense, had to be forgiven him, for he had been outrageously pampered by his mother. Poor Aunt Estelle worried over his seeing so much of his cousins. If only she had known how Rosanne and Colette really felt about her darling, she would have slept better at night, for they were far more interested in his possessions than in Octave himself.

Among other things, he had a portable organ, a radio transmitter, a jigsaw for cutting out picture puzzles, and even an altar of his own, before which he used to say Low Mass with Rosanne and Colette as his ill-trained acolytes.

Generous, dear Octave, thought Rosanne and Colette; the very model of all misunderstood and laughable cousins. And without the least bit of malice, they took advantage of him whenever it suited them to do so.

Another guinea pig in those early experiments with romance was their young neighbor, Guy de la Roche. He was a year younger than they, rather short, and possessed of an irritating way of finding out just where they were whenever they tried to get away from him. He was very fond of them in spite of everything, and as a bribe to be invited on their independent jaunts he would generously offer them raspberries from his mother's garden. Colette and Rosanne gladly accepted the tasty fruit, and they let him tag along, especially when they needed a partner for tennis or croquet. The croquet court and set belonged to Guy's parents.

Then there was Jules, the handsome law student for whom every girl in the village had set her cap. Summer after summer he used to hang around Guy's sister May, a captivating dark-haired girl who encouraged his every attention. Jules used to make fun of Rosanne and Colette's silent admiration of him. Whenever he passed them on the street, he would glare like a savage, hungry wolf, and ask, "Do you still love me, you little red riding hoods?"

But Moïse had been theirs alone. They forgave him his Biblical name, his inarticulateness, and his rough manners, for no other reason than that he knew they existed. Nevertheless, it was not until July that year that they first realized that he existed, too, and then it was only by chance. For if Uncle Henri had not bought the strip of beach, they might never have noticed Moïse, hidden as he always was in the crowd of blue serge suits at Sunday Mass. But for the new beach in the Vadeboncoeur family, he would have remained just another young farmer at whom they might have glanced twice, but that would have been all.

One sunny morning Rosanne was waiting on the tennis court for Colette, who dashed up like a meteor, her white skirt billowing behind her. She was running so fast that she bumped into Rosanne before she could stop, and she was quite out of breath as she gasped out the news she was bringing.

"Can you imagine, Rosanne? Papa is buying a piece of land on the lake!"

"Take it easy, *ma chère,*" said Rosanne, trying to free herself from Colette's exuberant embrace and laughing at her enthusiasm. "You've already got as good a view of the water as you could ever want."

Rosanne swept her hand toward the horizon where the enormous lake lay placid in the sun, unrippled in the still July air.

Colette grew wistful. "Isn't it beautiful, our own Témiscamingue! It has just one fault: it isn't good for anything now that the railroad has put an end to navigation on it." She sighed disconsolately. "It's a pity. I can remember when the steamboats used to come up from Long-Sault. We would wait for them for hours, and then suddenly, just when we weren't watching, they'd loom into sight around the point where the old fort is. Then they'd sidle up to the pier as if they knew there would always be a crowd waiting to see them arrive. The whole village would turn out to welcome them, all dressed up and cheering. It was a magnificent sight. But now . . ." She looked at the vast expanse of shimmering water undisturbed by a single vessel. "It's all over. The railroad ruined our fun."

Not only could they no longer watch for the paddle-wheel steamboats, but Aunt Adèle would not let them swim. She felt that the lake was too deep, the shores too steep, and the bottom too slimy. Colette and Rosanne were sure she was just mimicking the concern of the village priest, Father Hébert about his flock parading up and down the Lake Road in bathing suits. So swimming was forbidden, and it was sheer torture for them on a hot day like this one.

"Come on, let's go!" Colette dragged Rosanne along behind her as she set off at a run to get their bathing suits from the house. "Papa is going to take us on a picnic at the new place."

"But where's the beach? On the Petit Lac, way up north?" Rosanne asked.

"Silly! On Témiscamingue, but in another cove, seven miles from here. Just wait and see, we'll have a cottage, a beach, a rowboat. Oh, Rosanne, what a wonderful summer we're going to have!"

Rosanne could only think that it was too good to be true. Already the summer was turning out to be far better than she had expected.

Colette was right. Uncle Henri, after painstakingly surveying the neighboring countryside, had become proprietor, together with his in-laws, Alphonse and Sylvio, of a sandy stretch of beach some distance from the village. It could be reached only by a rocky little road which meandered across fragrant, green meadows from one farm to another, through a field of clover and then along the base of a hillock where Rosanne and Colette saw seven fat cows clustered around their salt brick. It crossed a little bridge, and then two more, and then another three, which had been thrown across the dry streambeds, and eventually it emerged at the Joly farm, the prettiest section of which now belonged to the Vadeboncoeurs.

The two cousins were in a seventh heaven of bliss. No more of the formalities of village life; no more having to dress up in the afternoon to go to church for Evensong. Here they could be completely themselves, roaming, swimming, behaving any way they wanted. The moment they reached the beach that day, they put on their red wool bathing suits and were allowed to dash to the lake and plunge headfirst into the cold, clear water.

Here the lake was so wide that the view took one's breath away. They were in Quebec; five miles below them was Ontario. The sky was blue, as blue as the lake. Yet when the sun cast the long shadow of the forest over the water, there were emerald tints in it. A brown line marked the meeting of the horizon with the dark shafts of the firs, crisscrossed by birches like a trellis. Far to the left the lake was finally cut off by mountains fitting behind one another like pieces in a giant's picture puzzle. The long, wide beach was strewn with dead trees which water and sun had whitened, their forked roots stretching starkly in every direction.

"What do you think of it?" Colette asked as she sat down on her blue and white striped towel and buried her bare feet up to the ankles in the sand. "It's real wilderness, isn't it? Oh, we'll have such fun exploring it."

As the summer days slid quickly by, the cousins spent many hours at the new cottage. They basked in the warm sun or lay idly on their backs in the water, watching the puffy clouds drift over them to disappear behind the distant hills. On clear evenings there were picnics beside the lake, the lights of Haileybury, the nearest town, blinking in the distance. They tramped across the fields to visit nearby farmers. Inquisitiveness kept their noses glued to a dusty windowpane as they watched a calf being born in a neighbor's barn. Together they stole the most delicious gooseberries in the world from Lawyer Bourassa's garden, and ate them behind his hedge, since the old widower would let the fruit rot rather than give it away. "You know," Colette said with her mouth full of the pale green, plump fruit, "if every sin is as pleasant as this, Father Hébert is wasting his time worrying about the salvation of the human race."

They wanted to be someone and do something important. One morning, after a sermon that made them realize their obligations to charity, they went to a poor family on the far side of the village, with their penny banks and a heap of old rags, to offer money and to help clean house. Two years later, Colette and Rosanne could still feel the warm, greasy water in which their enthusiasm drowned along with a vast number of flies. Colette in her white tennis dress had innocently asked how she should pick up the whimpering baby to put him into the tub. Aunt Adèle had smiled when they came home that night exhausted, disappointed by the indifference of the family, and cured for the time being of the need for such idealistic gestures. It was a half-sympathetic, half-satirical smile, which said more clearly than words, "And to think that here at home, you let the maid work like a horse and never even offer to dry a dish."

Rosanne loved Colette the way one loves a dear younger sister. She was only six months older than Colette, but felt far more mature. Life had not been easy for Rosanne. Her mother, a widow with three children, barely earned a living as a dressmaker. Rosanne, as the oldest child, became her mother's companion and confidante. The loss of her father, and the consequent daily economies the family had to practice after being used to all the material comforts, had made her grow up very early. Rosanne saw much that her mother hoped she would not have to see, whereas Colette, the youngest of her family, had been protected and often spoiled.

Colette and her sisters had gone to boarding school in Ottawa as a matter of course. The Sisters of the Congregation, in Gloucester Street, taught the children of the wealthy families, and going to their school was the proper thing to do. There Rosanne's cousins learned music and painting and other accomplishments without, she thought, much enthusiasm.

Rosanne went to the public primary school in her neighborhood in Montréal. Then after much hard work and careful saving, her mother had been able to give her a wonderful present—a year as a day student at a well-known boarding school in the city.

It was hard for Rosanne's mother to part with her for the summer, for Rosanne helped with the work and relieved her loneliness. But when Aunt Adèle wrote, "We would like to borrow your Rosanne for a while," her mother always answered: "Of course you may; she will be delighted." Dear Mamma, Rosanne would think as she said good-by, in such joy over a summer in Ville-Marie that she was ashamed of her selfishness.

During the winter the two cousins led different lives, but in Ville-Marie, they were summer sisters. They never thought of questioning an affection that was so natural, so spontaneous. It was simply the way that they felt and that was all the explanation they needed. They were cousins, and if they thought about it at all, it was just to think how nice and convenient it was that there was such rapport between them, even extending to Moïse.

Chapter 5

Moïse Joly, who had originally owned all the land of which the Vadeboncoeur beach was part, had kept a right of way to the water for the use of his sheep, horses and cows. Colette and Rosanne had played Marie Antoinette on his farm, which they envisioned as an enormous Trianon. They amused themselves by teasing the bull with a red handkerchief, snatching away from the cows the skirts which they seemed determined to eat, bleating the incessant baa-ing of the sheep back at them.

That first summer at the lake the field had to be cleared. To do the job Uncle Henri sensibly hired Moïse Joly, for the young man would feel he was still working on his own land. Moïse lived with his widowed mother in a little house with dormer windows. Its gray weathered exterior cried through all its thirsty pores for a coat of paint it would in all likelihood never get.

Colette and Rosanne were on the beach whenever the weather was good. In order to shield them from the sun and also provide a shelter in which to change their clothes, Uncle Henri set up a framework of rough boards over which he draped the largest of his surveyor's tents.

Colette and Rosanne asked every morning, "May we go to the bay today?"

Aunt Adèle would use her work as an excuse for not taking them, but eventually, as they kept insisting, she allowed them to go with Henriette. Marilou gladly surrendered this privilege of the eldest in favor of her hammock under the trees and her pile of French novels.

Henriette already had a driver's license, a great achievement in Colette's eyes, for Uncle Henri was very strict about letting his daughters drive. Rosanne and Colette admired her for it; they knew the battle she had fought to get it. Henriette, so gentle and meek and shy, was really the most persistent of all the cousins. Marilou with her pretty face and Colette with her vivacious ways sometimes tended to eclipse her, but in getting her own way, sensible Henriette was often the most successful.

Every time Uncle Henri went surveying along the Solitaire River or into the back country, he would get Henriette to drive him, and then turn the automobile over to her. A car plus Henriette inevitably equaled a trip to the bay.

Therefore, Colette and Rosanne had plenty of chances to watch Moïse who worked all through the summer clearing the field back of the beach. In his faded blue shirt and his dark blue jeans, he was handsome as only a man who has worked outdoors all his life can be. His high laced boots showed off his muscular legs; his shoulders were broad and powerful; and he stood tall and straight. They had eyes for him alone, and they pitied the two older girls' more sophisticated friends, college boys who talked about nothing but hockey, sports cars, and the like. Rosanne and Colette wanted a man "with eyes like the doves by the rivers of waters . . . hands as gold rings . . . countenance as Lebanon, excellent as the cedars." To them Moïse was the Bridegroom of the Song of Solomon, his hair smelling of the breezes that swept the meadows, in his clothing all the perfumes of the earth. They reveled in this image, yet they vaguely felt he was a man of real flesh and blood, too. It made no difference to them that Moïse could just barely read and write. His healthy good looks were quite enough. He was much older than they; yet he acted shy and awkward whenever he met them.

They used to watch him work, urging his horse by voice and gestures to tug at the stubborn tree stumps being cleared from their new land. Colette and Rosanne watched these struggles, applauding every success and saying much to each other, but never an actual word to Moïse. They were properly brought up young ladies, and he was a farmer who had not even been introduced.

Several times he started toward them as if to speak, but he never quite made it and merely went back to his stump-pulling: "Come on, Jocrisse, pull!"

"Listen to that," Colette whispered to Rosanne. "Not a bad name, for a horse. The man has wit." Then to him she said very rapidly, as if she were afraid she might change her mind, "Your horse has a funny name. Isn't Jocrisse the traditional simpleton of our French theater?"

That broke the ice. He turned to them, a broad smile on his face. Oh, how good-looking he was, they both thought.

"I wouldn't know, Mam'selle. It was the name of an admirer of my mother's, and my father thought it would be a good joke to call the horse after him. It was his way of getting even."

Then without pausing, and as if he wanted to please them but was afraid of offending, he asked, "Would you like to ride him while I'm working?"

It was just what they wanted. They had never been on a horse in their lives, and yet here they could guide one, talk to one, and—it seemed very likely—even touch the fingers of the handsome boy who would help them up on the horse's back.

Jocrisse seemed enormous as they stood beside him. Colette, who was bolder than Rosanne, went first. Was Moïse going to lift her up in his arms? Rosanne wondered enviously. Colette held her breath, but Moïse was too respectful to do more than lead the animal to the nearest stump, from which she could easily climb on its back.

Soon they were to owe him an even more intoxicating thrill. It happened the week the whole family camped out in the tent on the beach.

"Please go and get some milk at the Joly farm," Aunt Adèle asked them, the first night they arrived.

They dawdled along the path between the mounds of cut hay, while Colette chased grasshoppers, which she would hold in her cupped hands, whispering, "Give me your molasses, pray." Rosanne gathered wildflowers for a bouquet —daisies, satin-petaled buttercups, pale purple thistles—even though the family laughed at her every time she brought them back.

There was no one at home in the shabby Joly house. The flies were swarming around the open door and buzzing over the dented milk cans set out to dry in the shed. On the veranda two empty chairs with faded cushions kept each other company. There was a languor in the atmosphere; the dusk was beginning to hide the fields heavy with crops awaiting harvest. A thrush sang melodically, and the frogs in the pond croaked in answer to it.

Colette, who doted on all living things suggested that they go look at the ducks, but they had been shut inside their coop for the night.

"Well, we can look at the pond anyway," Rosanne said philosophically.

They lay flat on their stomachs in the warm sand at the edge of the pond, plunging their arms up to the elbows in the cool water, trying to touch the tadpoles and giggling at the frantic way the thin black tails wiggled, propelling the round bodies.

Moïse, his day's work done, was coming home along the road, leading his sweating horse by the reins.

"Well," he said as he saw Colette and Rosanne, "if it isn't the two young ladies." His face broke into a smile as he added, "*My* young ladies."

He looked them over from head to toe, without being

bold, yet with obvious pleasure. What the clear water of the pond had suggested to them, they now saw confirmed in Moïse's eyes. They were not hard to look at, even though they were wet and muddy, and dressed in their old clothes, Colette with her tanned skin, her black eyes, her curly hair tied with a red ribbon, her plump figure, her stubborn smile; and Rosanne quite like her but more shy and subdued, and with a dimple in her chin, of which she was vaguely ashamed.

"I bet you'd like a little canter," Moïse said as he led Jocrisse up to drink from the pond.

"Have you got a saddle?" Colette asked—a roundabout way of accepting the offer.

"No, but you'll do without one. Coming?"

"Well, you can't miss what you never had," Colette laughed, using one of her father's favorite expressions. "Are you coming, Rosanne?"

Rosanne had always been something of a coward, and she admired Colette for taking this risk so blindly.

"You go first," she said.

Then, suddenly, there was Colette astride Jocrisse. She had mounted with the help of a convenient fence post. There was a proud, triumphant expression on her face as she shouted, "What are we waiting for? Give me the reins, and swat this old nag on the rump!"

Moïse did not stir. "Do you know how to guide a horse?"

"Nothing to it! I've already been riding your old swayback for a month."

"But only when he's been pulling stumps in the field. Do you know how to turn him around to get back?"

Colette shook her head.

"In that case, wait a minute. I'm going to get on him, too," Moïse declared, and Colette gave Rosanne a mischievous look as he leaped onto the horse's broad crupper.

Off they went, walking at first, then trotting. Colette's legs flapped against the horse's flanks, and she was leaning back on Moïse, who was holding the reins on either side of her body. Rosanne began to worry about what Aunt Adèle would say if she were to see them. Still, she knew perfectly well she was going to do the same thing.

The riders came back in good condition. Colette's hair was wind-blown, her face was flushed. Rosanne waited without saying a word, ready to take to her heels in misery if they went on toward the little bridge without paying any attention to her. But Moïse held out his hand to her.

"It's Mam'selle Rosanne's turn now."

"My turn!" She was shaking with fear, but she would not have turned back for anything.

"Up you go, *ma petite!*" Moïse said. A click of the tongue, a "giddap," and Jocrisse was off, carrying Moïse and Rosanne.

She felt suspended between heaven and earth and hung on to Jocrisse's russet mane for dear life. Moïse had his arms about her, and she leaned her trembling body against his solid warmth. The horse was pounding the ground, and each hoof beat vibrated through every vertebra of her spine. And the thump of the hoofs echoed the heartbeats of Moïse against her back. Rosanne was caught up in a swirl of emotions. Free of whatever fear she had had, she burst out with a laugh which the wind drove back down her throat. Her curls were streaming out behind her, slapping at Moïse's face till he grabbed them and held them to his cheek.

"How soft your hair is," he said, "and how good it smells."

It was an exciting, wonderful apprenticeship to romance. Every evening during that unforgettable week, the two girls went for another riding lesson, without once revealing to the family the progress they were making. But when the truth came to light—Aunt Adèle went looking for them one evening—the scoldings were severe.

"Pooh!" Rosanne said to Colette, intuitively sure that in the same circumstances her aunt herself would have acted no differently.

Uncle Henri went straight to the point: "I forbid you to get on that horse or, what's more, to visit the farm or even to see that maniac again."

That was the end to the happy carefree episode. They saw Moïse only at High Mass on Sundays; and then, alas, out of his work clothes, and dressed like anyone else, he lost his fascination.

Then, one day, they met him by chance. It was a broiling afternoon toward the end of August, and Colette and Rosanne had gone alone together for a swim at the bay. Aunt Adèle had protested—it was still as much as their lives were worth to get her permission—but she was in no mood to argue on such a hot day, and they had been very persistent.

Under the blazing sun the walk seemed endless, and they flopped down to rest in the shade of a big pine tree.

In the distance they could see the lake glittering like a mirage.

On the porch of a nearby farmhouse sat an old woman with her arms crossed as if she were rocking a baby to sleep. A flaxen-haired girl was playing before the house. The barn was so full that the grain was spilling out of the door like an offering to the reaped fields that had provided it.

"Let's go in," Rosanne said, "I'm dying of thirst."

Colette only hummed illogically in reply, "Oh! if my lover would only come by." Uncle Henri had some skill as an amateur magician, and she must have inherited some of his powers; for as if she had conjured him up by witchcraft, Moïse suddenly passed them. "Passed" is exactly the right word for it. He did not stop. He just kept going along at a quick trot, driving a colt that was taking the rise of the hill in long strides. A wave to them, a crack of his whip, and he was nearly gone.

"Hey, we're going to the bay," shouted Colette. "Our feet are tired. Take us in your cart, please, Moïse."

Colette's voice was as sweet as a spoonful of honey. Still he hesitated. He stared at the narrow seat, scratched his head under the straw hat, estimated with a glance the distance he yet had to go, and finally consented, but with ill grace.

"Come on, climb up."

The light wagon jiggled and bounced over the stony road. They sat close together, soon gossiping like old friends, lamenting Uncle Henri's strict order, recollecting the horseback rides in the summer dusk.

When the family drove to the beach to pick up Colette

and Rosanne at the close of the day, however, they made the mistake of describing their impromptu ride.

"You little wretches!" groaned Aunt Adèle. "Do you know what that Joly boy had under the seat of his wagon?"

"A corpse?" Colette laughed. She could not understand her mother's distress, and she was still bouncing to the rhythm of Jocrisse's hoofs, leaning against a strong body that smelled of earth, tobacco and hair tonic.

"A corpse, indeed! It might well have been your own."

"I can't see that we did anything bad," Colette said irritably.

"Neither can I," Rosanne added out of loyalty, though she was not in the habit of arguing.

Colette put her hands on her hips. "The key to the mystery, it seems to me, is what was in that box under the seat. What could he have had in it? Bootleg whiskey? Loot from a burglary? Or plague germs?"

"What was in it?" Aunt Adèle raised her arms to heaven as if to ask what she had done to be visited with such misfortune. "What was in it? Oh, nothing at all, really. The whole village knew about it. Just a case of dynamite!"

Chapter 6

THE NEXT YEAR the invitation to Rosanne for a summer
with the Vadeboncoeurs had not come. Doubtless, Rosanne
had thought, Colette could do without her companionship
now that she had the doctor; and doubtless Aunt Adèle
had her hands full enough with three lovesick daughters—
Henriette and Marilou were engaged in husband-hunting—
to want to be bothered with a niece. Consequently, Rosanne,
who longed to be in the country for at least part of the
summer, had gone to visit another aunt on Calumet Island.

Her world broadened enormously there, and she acquired innumerable new experiences in that anthill of sports-
loving cousins, five boys who were full of energy and fond
of fun.

She learned how to ride a bicycle by getting on and
whizzing down a hill before she knew how to put on the

brakes. Her cousins picked her up and she started all over again.

She learned how to paddle a birchbark canoe, rotating her paddle like an eggbeater as she was swept into rapids by the current; how to land a fish that wriggled at the end of her line like a hanged man; and how to recognize the calls of woodpeckers and owls, though earlier the only birds she could identify were sparrows. She mastered swimming and diving. She made ice cream in an old-fashioned freezer. Best of all she learned how to carry on conversations with boys without getting embarrassed. But she still used to blush at the slightest provocation, for she was incapable of hiding her feelings, and her blushes always revealed them relentlessly.

"Attaboy, Rosanne," her cousins would say, for they had been reared in the English tradition by their Scotch father and French-Canadian mother. "You're a good sport." Then, to tease her, they would add, "We'll make something out of you yet: give us five or six years."

The boys had no silly prejudices against girls, and readily welcomed into the clan their unskilled cousin, so eager for their companionship. With them she served a good apprenticeship in getting along with others.

Meanwhile Grandmamma kept writing that Colette and the doctor . . . the doctor and Colette . . . and Rosanne's mother would pass the letters on to her so she could have news of her cousin. "True, Colette is only fifteen," Grandmamma would write, "and the doctor is a good ten years older than she. Still it's a fine combination, something we could scarcely have dreamed of in a dreary little village like ours, and, what's more she loves him."

She loved him. That was what counted. Grandmamma was Colette's ally against her parents, Uncle Henri and Aunt Adèle, who were quite opposed to such a disparity in age. But that was not really so astonishing, for Grandmamma, who, at sixteen, had married a widower old enough to be her father, had had a happy life.

In her sentimental way, Rosanne jealously collected the remarks she heard about the doctor and sealed them in her heart. Did anyone say he was sympathetic and conscientious? Rosanne knew he was. His patients loved him? So did she, even though she had never set eyes on him. Did he want to buy the drugstore and make it his office? Then she would live in Ville-Marie the rest of her life and help him mix prescriptions.

It would be extremely easy, thought Rosanne, for him soon to exhaust all the possibilities in Ville-Marie. When a bachelor settles in a village and has neither wife nor fiancée, a year is certainly time enough for him to discover a girl to marry. If he has not done so by then, it must be because the village girls don't suit him well enough to coax the spark into a flame.

"If he could only see me," Rosanne would think, sure of her power, "the spark would kindle a furnace."

Out of shyness in talking with others, Rosanne, ever since she was a child, had held long conversations with herself. In these imaginary dialogues she would always confound her opponents with her brilliance. Their replies would serve as a springboard for her own wit. People used to say, "Rosanne is up on the moon again."

But she would only put on her haughtiest manner and return to the world of her dreams. Now she had the habit of daydreaming about the doctor and it was too pleasant a one to change.

"When I get to Ville-Marie," she would say to herself back in Montréal after the summer was over, "I will be something new on the scene, a city girl. He will be charmed with me."

Still, she was not completely vain. She knew her weaknesses, or thought she did. Her family was poor. There would be no lavish dowry. But she was attractive, with a young girl's slender body; and she had brown hair which she wore in curls that bounced with the slightest movement she made. Her eyes were dark and soft, and her even, straight teeth flashed every time she smiled, which was often.

Her mamma quickly suspected what was brewing inside her head, and warned her about so premature and unrealistic an affection.

"If you ever want to be happy, Rosanne," she said, "don't run after happiness. The most unhappy people are the ones who have only happiness as their goal. Believe me, dear. I know."

But it was too late. Rosanne's course was already set, and she was thinking of the doctor as if he were hers. In her heart he was, and there no one could take him away from her. Not even he himself. At night she would bury her head in her pillow and shut her eyes to see him more clearly, and whisper, "This summer, I shall see your face. Oh, if summer would only come!"

Well, it had come, and Rosanne had met the doctor. He was everything she had dreamed he would be—a little shorter, maybe, but who cared?—and those words "I love you," sweet as ripe peaches, seemed to have been made to say to him. Now, she could settle into the slow rhythm of summer in Ville-Marie.

Chapter 7

THE FIRST WEEK, Colette and Rosanne were inside the house only to eat and sleep. The outdoors was always calling to them, and they were so hungry for fresh air that they often slept out on the balcony.

"No walls for us tonight," Colette would say, "we're sleeping under the stars."

She dragged the folding cots down from the attic, and Uncle Henri lent two of his sleeping bags, while Aunt Adèle dug out some old striped blankets. Colette closed the door to the balcony behind them to shut out the noises from inside, and they lay on their backs, studying the stars, though the eaves cut off a piece of the Big Dipper. The sky would often be veiled with fast-moving transparent clouds, while the light breeze rustled the leaves of the willow hedge. Far away, they could hear the monotonous ripple of the lake against the shore. They talked in whispers, as if in church, until their eyes closed. Then they slept soundly till dawn.

There was an air of expectation about those early mornings. A kind of golden mist hung in the air, as they listened to the din of the bells on the cows being driven to pasture by old Baptiste, who supplied much of the village with milk. Slowly everything emerged in the brightening light, as clear and fresh as if they had never seen it before. Their hearts beat faster as the excitement of the new day touched them.

The angelus bell would drift up from the village.

"Are you going to Mass?" Colette would ask.

She would turn on her shoulder and look sleepily at Rosanne through her dark eyelashes, not knowing quite what answer she wanted, sometimes hoping for the "no" that never came. For whenever they slept out of doors, they always went to Mass.

They loved to hurry along the shore of the lake, glistening so in the newborn day that it dazzled their eyes. The houses were still quiet beneath their gables; the birds sang at the tops of their voices; from the fields bordered by irrigation ditches drifted the scent of new-mown hay.

They ran their hands over the tops of the clipped hedges, snatching at a honeysuckle blossom, rising on their toes to grab a branch of a weeping willow or the lower leaves of an elm. Lawyer Bourassa's hedge was always the most neatly trimmed; its neatness was his delight, but it seemed that every day, a new morning glory vine would twist over its level top for no other purpose than to vex him and give the girls a blue flower for their dresses.

It was not hard to pray in the old church of Ville-Marie, under the long shadow cast on the light-colored wall by the lance of a plaster Saint Michael. The church smelled of candle grease and wax polish, and the worm-eaten pews creaked every time people knelt. A few prie-dieu were upholstered in tattered red velvet; others were of black leather, cracked and peeling with age. The girls always chose the velvet ones, which were easier on their knees.

Between the choir's responses she could hear birds outside, the cartwheels rumbling and the clomp of the horses' hoofs as they crossed the covered bridge over the creek, climbed up the hill and trotted by the church.

Every other day Uncle Alphonse sang Mass. Their grandmother was always there in her pew, interrupting the solemn prayers with her coughing. The cousins walked back to Castel Riant with her, Colette carrying her missal and Rosanne holding a silk sunshade over her head; and more often then not, she asked them to breakfast, an invitation they never refused.

Rosanne always had a special feeling about Sunday morning, when the family would go to church together in the car, and was always late. On the mornings after they slept outside, she and Colette often got there before the altar-boy did. But on Sundays everything was different. Then, church was an obligation, and Colette and Rosanne had to be yanked out of the bed by the feet or the ears or the hair.

The first Sunday in July was no exception.

Everyone wanted to use the bathroom at the same time.

"It's my turn," Marilou shouted from her bedroom.

"But I haven't finished shaving," Uncle Henri protested, sticking his lathered chin out the door.

Aunt Adèle called from downstairs, where she was watering her plants while waiting for them, "Hurry up! The fifteen-minute bell just rang."

Uncle Henri bellowed in outrage, his pajama coat hanging open above his trousers, "The sexton is fast, at least half a minute fast."

The bathroom was a large one, and the cousins could all get into it together. Colette washed herself just as her cat did, thoroughly and delicately. Marilou powdered her nose before the big mirror, leaving Rosanne only a corner of it in which to see to comb her hair, while Henriette brushed her teeth with methodical care.

Again from below came the impatient voice, "Listen, that's the last bell. Lord save us, it's shameful the way the Vadeboncoeurs always have to sneak in right in the middle of the Epistle."

Aunt Adèle was right. Once they got to the church, they had to climb up to the organ loft, Uncle Henri giving the sexton, his gnarled hands still clinging to the bell rope, a dark look as he passed him. They shoved their way as best they could through the farm hands who crowded by the door, waiting only for the first word of the sermon to make a dash for the porch where they smoked and awaited the end of the preaching.

The women were all in their best. High Mass on Sunday

in Ville-Marie produced a veritable extravaganza of costume, and revealed everyone's social status.

"Did you notice Joséphine Salvail's lace collar?" Colette whispered as she leaned over the railing of the loft to see better. "I saw one just like it at Woolworth's in Montréal."

Rosanne nudged her, but nothing could stop Colette from talking, no matter where she was. In church, Rosanne kept quiet, for she liked the still atmosphere and the murmur of prayers being offered in unison. It was as if a cloak were enfolding the entire village, offering a sanctuary for all the many longings, thoughts, and desires of the people.

The farm families stayed together in one group, as if to make a common front against the more well-to-do and prominent citizens. Their children wore old-fashioned clothes—the boys in the black suits and shining ankle-high boots in which they had made their first communion; the girls in cotton dresses that were too long for them, and round straw hats pulled down to their eyebrows. The disarming faces that peeped from under the brims, the wide smiles and the bright, curious eyes fascinated Rosanne. But Colette turned up her nose at them, saying, "Phew! They smell of sour milk."

The cousins endured the long sermon stoically. The Oblate Missionary Fathers who officiated at Ville-Marie were on the whole good preachers. Father Hébert was the most experienced and respected of them, and justly so, for he had been a missionary to the Canadian Indians and his sermons could arouse Christian sentiments in even the ignorant and the uncaring. His satirical tirades used to entertain at the same time they pricked the conscience.

He stroked his thick gray beard or slapped his bald, tanned forehead when he wished to emphasize a point. His turned-up nose was too large and his beard made his fleshy lips seem redder than they were, yet no one thought of poking fun at him. He always had a moment to spare for the young people in the village, and Rosanne never left Ville-Marie without going to say good-by to him. He had baptized her, and she felt that her devotion to him must have begun then.

There was always a dash of salt and spice in his sermons. Liars, misers, snobs, and drunkards were chastized harshly as his caustic tongue berated them in quick succession, painting their sins in vivid colors and demonstrating how concerned he was for the morals of his parish. The summer season brought back, along with the warm sunlight, his harangues against immodest dress.

Rosanne feared him and yet admired him as he waved his long arm toward heaven one Sunday, and thundered in indignation. "Our young people are becoming shameless," he intoned, looking from mother to mother. "The way they drive sixty miles an hour straight to perdition over the road to Petit Lac! When I speak of the perils that lie in wait for them along that road, I do not mean the hairpin curves alone. You know well enough what I have in mind."

His voice swelled with wrath: his shoulders towered above the pulpit on which he was pounding. His beard shook and the cross that hung from his cincture he brandished at first one, and then another girl, none of whom dared to look at him.

He censured the latest styles, too, particularly shorts, to the great despair of Marilou who had bought two pairs that she would never dare wear now, except at the beach.

Once the sermon was over, everyone in the congregation breathed a little easier. They discussed it as they were leaving the church, some approving, others condemning it.

"Does he have to be so strict?" the disappointed girls complained.

"He is right," their fathers replied. "He is protecting our children." They were ready to denounce the escapades of their own youth to impress on their daughters the need for virtue.

The sermon was Aunt Adèle's favorite topic of conversation at Sunday dinner. The meal was both breakfast and dinner and Rosanne ate greedily. Marilou's dish of baked pork and beans was the main course. She prepared it skillfully, using plenty of molasses and burying in the center an onion rubbed with dry mustard. On Saturday, the baker came in his wagon to take away the full beanpot and pop it into his oven along with his pans of bread. Then, after Mass on Sunday, the Vadeboncoeurs stopped on their way home to pick it up and to buy two loaves of bread fresh from the cooling table.

Usually, on Saturday night, Henriette made a spice cake and frosted it, marking the icing to indicate where Uncle Henri should cut the pieces. There was sweet butter for the still-warm bread, strawberries Colette and Rosanne had picked, and, to pour over the fruit, heavy cream, which Uncle Henri pronounced "cre-e-e-m" in such a savory way his niece and daughters always teased him. It was a solid meal suited to the family's provincial summer Sundays.

Afterward there was another repast—this time of music. The living room was transformed into a concert hall the minute Uncle Henri gave the signal: "Now, girls, to your instruments!"

Rosanne could never understand why he had to beg and cajole her cousins, for she was dying to be part of the orchestra. But she had never learned anything but a few of the simplest piano pieces, and had to sit with her arms folded while she yearned to be on the polished bench performing with the aplomb of a famous concert pianist.

"Today we shall try the 'Angel's Serenade,'" Uncle Henri said, as he took the violins out of the cupboard.

All three daughters protested: "Oh, no, Papa, not that! . . . Schumann's 'Träumerei,' if you must, or Mascagni's 'Intermezzo,' but not the 'Serenade.' . . . We've had enough of that old serenade."

Their father merely turned a deaf ear, and went on searching for the scores of the piece he had chosen. The 'Angel's Serenade' was the sort of thing he loved. He tenderly took his clarinet out of its case and tootled a few runs for practice. Marilou pouted over in a corner, longing to escape to the hammock under the trees and read. When she finally got out her cello, she wrapped her knees around it as if she wanted to throttle it. The sounds she drew from it were just like her mood—spiteful and sour. Then, little by little, she was drawn into the music, and by the time the final crescendo was reached, she was playing the best of them all.

Henriette was always ready and willing to play, for she liked her violin and, though it was clear she would never become a virtuoso, she performed agreeably.

Rosanne wouldn't have missed the family concert for the world. She sat on the sofa, with soft cushions piled behind and beside her. Above her hung a sample of Aunt Adèle's needlework, a picture in the style of Fragonard of a dimpled eighteenth-century shepherdess soaring in a swing above the head of her swain.

On the opposite wall were an engraving of Rouget de Lisle, composer of the "Marseillaise," and several water colors her cousins had done in school. Rosanne studied Monsieur Rouget, Marilou's still life, and the row of poplars leading to the windmill in Henriette's landscape. She knew each line by heart, for she had scrutinized them many times during these chamber-music sessions.

Alone on the sofa, she felt briefly ashamed of having no more talent than she had, and yet pleased that no one was demanding any effort on her part. She was free to daydream while her cousins were working hard to provide the atmosphere of romantic music that induced her reverie. She liked to think that before the audience of one, the artists were encouraged to play better, for after the first squeaky measures, the violin began truly to sing, the cello groaned less and less, and her uncle beamed.

"That's the stuff, my little tigresses! Now we are making progress!" he said.

Rosanne's cousins peered at her over their music racks

and winked at each other, as if to say, "Poor Papa, he still believes he is raising musicians."

But their looks also said, "Dear Papa, we can't help loving you, even if you do make us play this sentimental music."

Chapter 8

That summer, there were even fewer boys in Ville-Marie than usual. Uncle Henri's surveying assistant, Jean-Claude, had just been married. Jules, the law student who used to tease Rosanne and Colette had not returned to the village, having married the daughter of a rich family in the city. They suddenly found May, whose conceit used to irritate them so, quite companionable. Octave was now busily studying for the priesthood, and Guy, May's younger brother, had acquired a sheepdog, the better to trail them and spy on their secrets like a detective.

Marilou and Henriette were now almost eighteen and nineteen, and the summer held plenty of promise for them. Their beaux of the past two summers had faithfully come back to Ville-Marie for the long vacation, and were as attentive as ever.

Everything would have been wonderful if only there

had been, on Lake Street, two black Fords and two doctor Renauds. Colette did have an admirer, Paul, the baker's son, but she was rather unkind and let him do his admiring from a distance. She seemed to derive a certain pleasure out of her transparent—and unsuccessful—maneuvers to interest him in Rosanne, and vice versa.

Since their meeting before the grocery store, Rosanne had seen neither the Ford nor its driver. At Mass that morning, she had anxiously surveyed every inch of the church, but Yves was not there.

About two o'clock, when the musicale was over, Colette asked, "What shall we do?"

"What do you want to do now?"

Rosanne was feeling lazy, yet she did not want to waste the afternoon sprawling in one of the chintz-covered cane chairs on the cool porch, looking through the vines at whoever might stroll past. On such a sunny day the doctor might well be someplace where a proper young girl could just happen to meet him accidentally.

"How about going to the softball game?" Colette asked. "Ville-Marie is playing the English team from Témiscamingue, south of the lake. Papa is going to play, and so are Uncle Sylvio and Uncle René."

"Let's go," said Rosanne, leaping up from her chair.

Arm in arm and singing at the top of their lungs their own version of the "Marseillaise": *"Allons, enfants de Ville-Marie . . . ,"* they started up the hill to the fairground, which was sometimes used as a softball field. The sun was beating down mercilessly and when they arrived, there was no one in the hot bleachers. Children swarmed like mosquitoes about the players of the local team who were warming up on the bases. Bright-colored dresses spotted the side lines, and already there were empty soda bottles on the grass.

They sat down in the shade of the family Packard, which Henriette had parked behind the backstop, not far from home plate, when she had driven Uncle Henri to the field.

Casually, both Colette and Rosanne looked around for the doctor. There wasn't a Ford to be seen.

Henriette and her friend, Jean, who was so devoted to her it made all the girls envious, were sitting in the car.

"Why don't we go for a ride?" Henriette said to no one in particular. "It's hot and I'm tired of waiting for the game to start."

"Why not?" answered Jean, beaming. Then, turning to Rosanne and Colette, he added condescendingly, "You kids can come along with us. We'll go to the bay."

They accepted with delight, and drove off, moving slowly along the country roads, waving at the towheaded farm children they passed and singing rounds loudly and off key.

It was the first trip to their beach that year. The great expanse of blue water and yellow sand had never looked lovelier to them. Several square cottages, painted in gay colors, had sprung up along the shore of the lake, resembling neat building blocks on the stilts which raised them above the high-water mark. Their own cottage was unchanged, its porch swept clean, its neat rooms awaiting the girls whose arrival inevitably turned order into confusion, as they dumped their bathing suits, towels, sweaters and books and ran off to explore the beach.

The Joly farm, once so active, now was abandoned; and the wild grasses, no longer kept cropped by the animals, had grown over the path to the door and surrounded the porch with their clusters of green seed heads. All that remained of the garden were a few clumps of young corn.

It was sad to see the house shuttered and empty in the midst of the deserted fields and meadows filled with white daisies. After his widowed mother had remarried, Moïse had left the farm, and was said to be working in the gold mines up north in Abitibi. Rosanne pictured him wretchedly slaving hundreds of feet below the surface of the ground and dreaming nostalgically of his farm so far away.

"To think of our Moïse as a miner," Colette said. "Remember, Rosanne, how he used to love his fields and the fresh air and being his own master?"

Indeed she did remember. And how his hair used to blow in the wind, and the expression of pleasure on his tanned face as he gazed out over the lake, grateful for its cool breeze after a day of stump pulling. Neither of them would forget him easily.

While Henriette and Jean were writing love letters in the sand, Colette and Rosanne walked up on the porch to peer at the bare interior of the house. There was dust everywhere, and the place smelled of mice. The rain had streaked furrows through the grime on the windows, which they traced with their finger tips.

"Why do you suppose he left?" Rosanne asked, suddenly curious. "It took such a short time to change his life completely. Two years ago, we were riding on Jocrisse's back with him and we were all so happy and carefree. And what about you in the meantime?"

"I?"

Rosanne had not intended Colette to take her question seriously, but she did. She sat down on the porch railing and began to recount the chance encounters she and Moïse had the previous summer.

"Last year," she said slowly, "I saw him several times in the village. I would say good morning to him and ask how he was, and think no more of it. You see, I had Yves. The whole Moïse thing was nothing to me but a pleasant memory. Oh, Rosanne, do you suppose . . . do you suppose he was in love with me?"

She seemed so disconsolate that Rosanne was sorry about her bold question. But now she could see how hard it would have been for Moïse not to like Colette, so different from the farm girls he was used to, a girl who thought nothing of riding a farm horse bareback over the fields in her white tennis dress.

"Aren't you flattered," Rosanne said, "that a man gave up everything on your account?" For they were both sure now that Moïse had gone to the mines to get away from the girl he loved but could never have.

"Yes," Colette said wistfully, "of course I am. I wouldn't be much of a woman if I weren't. But I hope we're mistaken. I shouldn't want what happened to me with Yves to happen to Moïse. If only you knew, Rosanne, how painful it is to love someone who doesn't love you. How painful and how discouraging."

As if I cared, thought Rosanne impatiently. The important thing was that at last Colette had started to confide in her about the doctor. But suddenly Colette jumped off the porch and took to her heels, carrying her secret with her as she ran across the fields to the waiting car.

"Hop in, kids," ordered Jean. "Time to go."

When they got back to the baseball grounds, the game was almost over. The village team was ahead and the onlookers were cheering enthusiastically. With the exception of the one man at bat, the English team, tired and very warm, was sitting cross-legged on the grass.

"Three mens out!" yelled Uncle René, who was umpire. He ran the general store in the village, and his family was glad that his bookkeeping was better than his English.

The Ville-Marie team left the field, and was replaced by the visitors in their gray and red striped uniforms.

The ninth inning began.

Henriette parked the car and Rosanne and Colette leaned out of the windows to watch.

"See what I told you!" they suddenly heard a woman near them say. "When Doctor Renaud is playing, we always win. He's a champion."

Colette and Rosanne looked at each other with a sinking sensation in their stomachs. Here, the doctor had been playing all afternoon, and they had not even known it. Instead, they had wasted two hours idly driving about the country-side. What idiots they had been! There he was, on third base and looking as noble as any knight, even though he was in a baseball uniform and not in sleek chain mail. The pitcher hurled the ball. Yves streaked for home and made it. Safe!

He took off his cap to acknowledge the cheers of the spectators, and then, ignoring the several girls who were calling to him, headed straight for the Vadeboncoeur Packard like a homing pigeon.

A contagious smile spread over his usually sober face, as if it were a flag he was raising to salute them, and Rosanne was sure there was no one more magnificent as he stood there in his black and white uniform. She noticed the envious looks and knew the girls he had ignored could have easily sent the two cousins to perdition.

He leaned casually on the window frame of the car and laid his hand on Rosanne's elbow.

"May I dedicate that last run to you?"

His face was almost touching hers. His skin was damp with sweat, and his freshly shaved cheek looked so soft that she had to clasp her hands together to keep from touching it.

That morning she had tied her hair with a lavender ribbon. She took it off and gave it to him with a shy yet almost smug smile. He took her hand, turned it over to kiss the palm gallantly, and then held it in his own.

"Milady's colors will bring us victory."

Colette jealously ripped off her own hair ribbon and

pushed Rosanne aside to hand it to him. "Two colors are better than one. Now you'll win twice as fast," she said pettishly.

He laughed, and brushed the back of her hand with his lips. Uncle René was waving at Yves to return to the game, and he excused himself reluctantly.

"If both of you are going to be home this evening," he said, "I'd like to take you for a drive." Then he ran off like a young colt.

That evening Colette deliberately settled herself in the middle of the front seat, leaving the window seat for Rosanne, though in her own father's car she, being the youngest, and consequently the most indulged, always demanded that coveted outside position as her rightful one.

The doctor continually leaned across her to speak to Rosanne. "I'm the one he's interested in," Rosanne kept thinking. "I alone."

The threesome became a daily thing, as the doctor began to take Colette and Rosanne with him to call on his many patients. He nicknamed them his Florence Nightingales, and they certainly thought of themselves as angels of mercy the day they had to take a seriously injured man to the hospital, his hands in theirs as they leaned over the back of the seat to comfort him. Still Colette was always in the middle, and Rosanne on the outside.

In spite of the crusts of condescension her cousin tossed her, Rosanne lived for these drives, certain that in the eyes of the passers-by she was chaperoning a romance that was flourishing between the doctor and Colette. But one evening all that changed. Before her unscrupulous rival could slide into her usual place, the doctor took Rosanne's hand and said, "You get in first, Rosanne. Sit next to me."

"Oh, Yves, Yves," Rosanne wanted to murmur and shout at the same time. The doctor had shown his preference.

Her arm touched the rough tweed of his jacket and rubbed against it gently. Colette sank into a sullen silence which showed all too clearly how she felt, and would feel during the rest of the summer. Rosanne writhed with embarrassment every time her cousin gave her a little shove and told her to get into the car first.

"Since that's the way *M'sieu le docteur* wants it," Colette would say sarcastically, "we have to please him."

Colette was miserable. Now it was she who was the chaperone, not Rosanne. Clothed in authority, Aunt Adèle, remembering her own very strict convent upbringing, would say inexorably, "I absolutely forbid you two young girls to go riding in a car alone with a man, no matter who it is."

Marilou and Henriette could ignore that dictum because they were older, but not Rosanne and Colette. And on every ride, Rosanne's happiness was slightly spoiled by Colette's presence.

Chapter 9

THE VADEBONCOEUR FAMILY and all the relatives spent many evenings picnicking at the bay. Each of the aunts brought a heaping basket, which was placed in the center of the huge trestle table set up out of doors. Then everyone chose his favorite foods from among the special dishes of each family. Afterwards the aunts and Grandmamma cleared up, while the young cousins splashed around in the water, and the men pitched horseshoes.

In that quiet and remote part of French Quebec, bathing suits were still modest and conservative, revealing little even when they were wet, and only a few of the older men had exchanged their old-fashioned bathing suits with tops like undershirts for more modern garb. The first time Rosanne saw the doctor in his swimming trunks, she was surprised and a little touched. He seemed rather skinny for such a good baseball and tennis player. His slim body was covered with red spots which he tried to hide by keeping his arms folded across his chest. When he saw the way she stared at him, he laughed.

"Don't worry, Rosanne," he said. "I don't have measles or some loathsome disease. It's hives, and you're responsible."

"Don't be silly! How could I be?" she said, looking down at the sand.

"You and the strawberries you picked for me yesterday. They are really to blame. I'm sure I'm allergic to them."

"Well, I'm hardly responsible for the way wild strawberries behave."

"Don't worry. Fortunately, I am not allergic to Rosannes. Otherwise I would really have it in for you."

They teased each other and laughed a great deal, but Rosanne was beginning to feel that she was walking a tightrope strung across a chasm. She cast covetous eyes at Yves when she thought he wouldn't notice; then pretended coolness when he was with her. Actually, if he knew anything at all about girls—and it was increasingly obvious that he did—he could not help perceiving how she liked him. But how inexperienced her subterfuges proved her to be!

When Yves came into a room where she was, and looked into her eyes, a smile on his serious face, the day became a wonderful one. Until the moment he left, she felt alive and wanted; she watched and remembered his slightest gestures; she cherished the sound of his voice. So far, no one but Colette and Yves realized the depth of her infatuation.

She took great pains not to let the slightest action mar her reputation for being a charming young girl—the kind one brings home to mother. At the evening picnics, when, as soon as the last bit of dessert had been gobbled, the young people rushed off to play games—hide and seek, treasure hunts, broad-jumping contests—and some of the younger boys ducked into the trees to smoke sun-dried corn silk, Rosanne always stayed behind to scour the pots and pans. "Why, that sweet Rosanne," she could hear them saying, "so dutiful, so unselfish. See how flushed her cheeks are from working so hard."

"And from getting so many compliments for her helpfulness," Rosanne added. Her hair prettily escaped its ribbon, as she scrubbed away, half for the sake of the pot, half for her reputation. She was determined to be thought of as someone who would make a perfect little wife for a doctor.

Perhaps it was vanity, yet in all the airs she put on, there was a certain concession to the ideal Yves had inspired in her. She wanted to be absolutely perfect, so she could earn his love; and in this, she was sincere to the bottom of her heart.

Everything turned out the way she wanted and planned. She was held up as an example to her cousins, who could have cheerfully seen her drawn and quartered for her excessive zeal and for the odious comparisons that were made between them and clever Rosanne.

Once the dishes were picked up and the tables folded away, the families sat in a circle at the edge of the beach, while the bonfire blazed on the sand. It crackled and snapped, its beauty filling them with dreams as the logs burned slowly down to embers.

Aunt Adèle called to her husband, who was deep in a discussion with his friends and brothers-in-law. "Henri-pet," she cooed, "Henri-pet, come sit by me."

But Uncle Henri did not budge.

Then her softly wheedling tone became stern and her voice grew louder, "Henri!"

He kept on with his conversation without turning his head. He was waiting, as the rest of the family always did, for the third summons. Just as regularly as clockwork it came, loud and sharp and angry: "Charles-Henri!"

After that Charles-Henri could not refuse. He rose up meekly and came over to his wife, a sly smile creasing his cheeks.

"Did you call me, *ma mignonne?*"

At the far end of the lake the lights of Haileybury winked like distant fireflies. The picnickers stretched out on the warm sand in the summer darkness, some on their backs, others on their stomachs, and sang in harmony. The flaming colors of the sunset had faded and the sky was now black, studded with stars. Uncle Henri, who was something of an astronomer, pointed them out one by one, telling his daughters, nieces and nephews their names and their magnitudes.

The waves, invisible but for their white crests of foam, broke steadily on the shore and the upturned tree roots, hung with bath towels and bathing suits, seemed to sway in the light breeze like laden clotheslines. There was a shower of orange sparks whenever anyone threw another dry log on the fire.

The doctor moved over to where Rosanne was sitting, a sweater around her shoulders, and grasped her hand firmly in his own.

"Little girl of mine," he whispered.

"How handsome he looks," she thought, as the flickering firelight illumined the smooth planes of his face. She longed to touch his cheek, yet she did not dare break into his reserve. "What makes him so elusive?" she wondered. Knowing as little of her own nature as she did of his, aware only of the way she felt toward him, Rosanne searched blindly for an opening through which she could slip into his life and become indispensable to his happiness.

The voices of those who were dear to Rosanne were singing all around her. She banished them to the back of her mind, along with her mother of whom she studiously avoided thinking, so that she might devote herself, heart and soul, to Yves.

Into the calm night came the peaceful music of the hymn to the Virgin, led by Uncle Alphonse:

> *As the dewy shades of even*
> *Gather o'er the balmy air,*
> *Listen, gentle Queen of heaven,*
> *Listen to my vesper prayer!*
> *Holy Mother, near me hover,*
> *Free my thoughts from aught defiled;*
> *With thy wings of mercy cover*
> *Safe from harm thy helpless child!*

The earth was blending with the sky. Tears glistened in Rosanne's eyes as Yves gazed into them. She turned from him, glad that the darkness hid her face so that she might keep her true feelings from him.

Where now was Colette, whom she had called her sister and whom she was betraying? She existed no more, either for Rosanne or for Yves. In all the world there was none but the two of them so much in love, though not a word had been spoken, no sign made.

Yet Colette was there, sitting between her father and mother. Rosanne could glimpse her cousin's anxious profile, and she shriveled with shame. But it took only a moment to stifle that stab of remorse and rebound into lighthearted joy at having Yves hold her hand in the darkness. Rosanne no longer thought of what she was doing. She was content to be with Yves.

Chapter 10

THE CLEAR SKY was tailored to fit the long hours in the open and the fresh breeze from the lake and the blazing sun made every day a perfect one. The scent of sweet clover was constantly in the air. It was a summer made for gladness, and Rosanne was happy as she had never been before.

On the spur of the moment the cousins invented holidays and anniversaries, and wrung permission from their family for parties. Of all of them Rosanne was the most eager, the most determined to keep the days from moving toward September and the inevitable farewell to Ville-Marie.

One evening the Vadeboncoeur household celebrated the return to the fold of a long-departed member. Uncle Bill had emigrated to the States twenty years before and now he had come back to introduce three Americans—his wife, his daughter Eve, and his streamlined automobile—to his native village. They planned to rent a house and stay till

December, Uncle Bill's doctor having prescribed a long rest away from New York for his tired patient. Although vivacious Eve caused much comment, it was the long, light blue car that aroused the most; it was the only Cadillac in the village, and far too magnificent for conservative Ville-Marie.

The doctor had been invited to the party and so had Jean and Georges, a friend of Marilou's. May was there, too, with red-haired Luc, who was Jean's brother. Octave and Guy were present, both of them fascinated by Eve's long blond hair; and, of course Colette and Rosanne.

At intervals Aunt Adèle came into the living room and joined good-naturedly in the conversation, spoiling the fun a little. Her interruptions were forgiven, though, because with each appearance she passed more of the grape punch that glowed in the crystal glasses.

"Why don't we put on a show?" Marilou suggested. "Sort of an amateurs' night? It's the latest thing in town now, isn't it, Rosanne?"

Rosanne always spoke with authority about life in the city. Many of her remarks began with "in Montréal," and whenever they did, the rest would listen avidly to whatever she had to say.

"In Montréal? Oh, yes," Rosanne said pompously. "Amateur groups and charades are all the rage."

"Every party that's any fun has them," said Luc, eager to display his familiarity with cosmopolitan life."

"Well, why don't we?" said Marilou. "Who's with me?"

Everyone, when his turn came round, did some stunt or other. Eve began with a tap dance. Marilou added jazz to her everlasting "Boléro" and warmed that up for them; it was as dear to her heart as some old dress she couldn't bear to part with. Henriette played her violin with more inspiration than usual. Jean and his brother, who had just graduated from Mont-Saint-Louis, Montréal's best high school, where gymnastics were popular, walked around the room on their hands to the considerable peril of Aunt Adèle's potted ferns.

Everyone, from the smallest to the biggest, did something. May's parody of Maurice Chevalier—complete with tilted straw hat, cane, soft-shoe dance and nostalgic song, got the biggest laugh. May loved to clown, especially when she had an admirer in the audience. Then Colette played her concert piece, a mazurka, as if she were a schoolgirl performing for the Mother Superior.

The doctor squatted on a hassock waiting for his turn. Rosanne was praying no one would remember she was there.

"Now you, Rosanne," said Yves, who must have thought she was being saved for dessert like a chocolate éclair.

She tried a joke. "I'll have to beg off," she said. "I left my harp in Montréal. And, anyhow, all I can play is 'My dog has fleas.'"

"Come now, Rosanne," said Aunt Adèle, who was watching from the side lines, "you can sing, and very sweetly, too."

"Oh, no!" she gasped. She had never learned *solfeggio* or harmony. Why was Aunt Adèle putting her in the spotlight? Rosanne, who often missed notes in "Chopsticks," knew she could do nothing but underline the vast difference between herself and Colette, who was cultivated to the roots of her curly hair. Aunt Adèle, who had been so kind and hospitable, had inadvertently turned into a wicked stepmother.

"Come on, Rosanne, sing!" everyone insisted, not realizing that just the presence of Yves was enough to destroy her composure.

He, too, joined in the general urging. "What are you going to give us?" he asked.

"I don't know," she said in a panic.

"I know," said Colette, "the Chopin 'Nocturne,' the one with words. You were singing it yesterday coming home from the bay."

For a fleeting second, Rosanne loathed her cousin. The words of the song were a declaration of love.

To her added discomfort, Colette said, "I'll accompany you," and ran to the piano. Marilou moved to the record player to get out records to dance to later.

"I'm trapped," thought Rosanne with a sick feeling in her stomach. On the first line, her voice was off pitch and quavered dreadfully. Somehow she got through the next two lines. Then, her initial terror over, she began singing in full voice. Her eyes focused on a rose petal lying on the rug, while everyone else was gazing at her, motionless in the center of the room. The high G was waiting for her, grinning like a fiend, as she soared bravely on to disaster. She used to be able to reach that note feebly but accurately, or at least, so she thought. This time, it stuck in her throat and came out with a horrible squawk. The silence could have been cut with a knife. Marilou slowly opened the lid of the phonograph. Rosanne somehow got control of herself, and pushed on to the end of the song.

Then she slunk toward the sofa to disappear into its cushions. With a thunderous crash she sat down on a pile of old records, smashing them to pieces.

That, it seemed, was screamingly funny—for the others. The laughter that had been repressed during her wretched performance was restrained no longer, and it flared around her like firebrands in a dry forest.

Rosanne felt she was living a nightmare, worse than when her father had taken her years ago to the Chamber of Horrors in Dominion Park in Montréal. It had been all right to cry then, because she was so young, but now she would have died before she let any of them see tears. Yet to cry bitterly was all she felt like doing.

As Rosanne sat there in the middle of the sofa, she could see Aunt Adèle mentally calculating the damage. The records had been a valuable collection of Glenn Miller and other bands of the 'thirties that were saved for special parties.

"She's as red as a boiled lobster!" gasped Eve, catching her breath from laughing.

"Lobster à la Newburg!" added one of the boys.

If Rosanne could have sunk through the floor, she would never have come up again till Judgment Day, but the floor refused to co-operate.

"Come on, Rosanne; don't just sit there," Marilou ordered. "Get up so we can pick up the pieces." She was none too pleased at the damage, especially at the loss of her favorite record, "Red Sails in the Sunset."

"What can I do? Where can I hide?" was all Rosanne could think of. She was sure she would never get over the shame, so much worse since Yves had seen her blunder. She felt as forlorn as the Little Match Girl whom she hadn't thought of since she was nine years old and last heard the story.

Yves stood up and said to the group, "I'm going to get a box of chocolates at my drugstore for everyone who took part."

"Go ahead," laughed Marilou, "and bring back all the other stuff you haven't sold." Then she whispered to May, "What's come over him? He's so generous all of a sudden."

He took Rosanne by the hand and pulled her to her feet. "Come help me," he said.

Rosanne suddenly felt as if she'd been saved from disaster. She no longer cared anything about the others, especially Eve, who would have liked to have been chosen. She hurriedly left the room, determined to devote the rest of her life to making Yves happy in gratitude for his gesture.

Once they were in his car with the doors shut, he turned to her. He smiled affectionately.

"Now, at last, I can have you to myself for a moment. It took a lot of waiting to get this."

He raised her chin gently so that he could look at her. "Rosanne, for whom did you sing the Chopin?"

"Hah, what did I tell you," her intuition whispered to her. "Yves is not a fool. He knows."

"Did you like it?" she said, and waited in suspense for his answer, for she could think of nothing else to say.

"Those words you sang—'my heart devotes its song to you'—did you really mean them?"

He looked straight into her eyes. There was such gentleness in his face, such sincerity in his smile, that her embarrassment and chagrin disappeared. She settled back against the car seat in relief, and smiled at him without a word. Silence seemed the only adequate way to respond, far better than any awkward phrases she might find.

"Why don't you answer?" he said. "Not that it matters. I can wait. I can be very patient when I think it worth while to be."

"Thanks," she said in a low voice, "for waiting for me."

The motor was racing, and he obviously did not hear those words full of meaning.

"I'm taking tomorrow night off," he said. "The doctor is going on strike and taking Rosanne to the movies in Haileybury. It's 'Gone With the Wind.'"

"We're going alone?"

Rosanne was overjoyed that he should have suggested it. But she was dreaming of the impossible; Aunt Adèle would never allow it, and she would not go against her aunt's wishes.

"Why not?" he said. "Don't you trust me?"

"I'd go to the ends of the earth with you." Rosanne closed her mouth with a gasp at her daring, for they both knew that she meant it.

He laughed. "And yet you won't go fifty miles from here with me. Your earth is rather small, it seems to me. Well, suppose we take Colette, too; and Aunt Reine, whom I adore; and your cousin Eve, whose fifteenth birthday it is; and the cat and the dog and the goldfish and Father Hébert."

"Now you're going too far. Leave out Father Hébert and the zoo, and keep the others, and we'll go."

"You're adorable, Rosanne." Then, with a light laugh that almost robbed his words of meaning, he added, "And I adore you."

At last, she had heard him say the words she had dreamed of. . . .

And the next evening his caresses were so sweet, so unexpected that they left her trembling in the dark. They were coming home from the movies, and the country roads were deserted. It was very late, and there was no moon. The car gave a gasp and refused to proceed. Yves stopped to let the engine cool, and turned out the lights. In the sudden blackness and quiet, they could hear the crickets chirping in the grass.

Aunt Reine dozed in the back seat. Eve slept beside her, her head on her aunt's lap. Colette was cat-napping next to Rosanne in the front seat, leaning on the open window frame.

Rosanne began to daydream again. Were Yves' words of the night before part of her dream, or were they a reality? She knew no longer what to think. Rosanne was very conscious of the solid warmth of Yves' body next to hers, but they were enveloped by the darkness, and could not see each other's faces.

The doctor raised her hand to his lips. Slowly he kissed her fingers one by one, then turned her hand to press his mouth against first the back and then the palm. Rosanne leaned against him and did not move, sure she could not, even if she had wanted to.

From time to time, Aunt Reine asked, "What do you think the trouble is? Can't we get going again soon?"

Yves answered in a strange voice; it was at if a frog were caught in his throat. A few moments later his arm came around Rosanne's shoulders, and he pressed her to him, his mouth sweeping across her cheek until it found her lips. Instinctively she turned away.

In a torment of indecision she wondered why, when she wanted nothing so much in all the world as to be kissed by him. Was she afraid? "Afraid of Yves? No, that couldn't be." It was the kiss itself she feared, not Yves. It took her by surprise. She was not ready for it, even though she had been longing for it.

He took his arm from her shoulders. "Have I offended him?" she asked herself anxiously. He had been so attentive, and now she was refusing him such a simple thing, the only thing he had ever asked of her.

"Are we off?" Colette asked, suddenly sitting up.

"Yes, we're off," the doctor said as he started the car.

"It's about time!"

So softly no one but Rosanne could hear him, Yves whispered in her ear, "Don't forget. I can be very patient."

Chapter 11

WHAT WAS BOUND to happen sooner or later, did happen. Colette asserted herself. One evening the doctor, looking quite dashing in his everlasting gray jacket and white flannel trousers, stopped in to invite Rosanne and Colette to a play ten miles from Ville-Marie. The two girls were alone in the house, practicing duets on the piano.

"Hurry up," he ordered them. "It's late. I've got front-row seats and I bet they're between those two old potbellies, the deputy and the mayor."

Rosanne accepted his invitation without a moment's hesitation and raced up the stairs to change out of her shirt and khaki skirt. Her yellow silk suit would be perfect, she knew. It was the treasure of her wardrobe and Mamma's masterpiece. Dear, dear Mamma, with your magic needle, she thought. I will write you tonight; no, not tonight, tomorrow.

Rosanne was suddenly stricken by her lack of gratitude. Her mother had denied herself in order to send her, a few days before, a wonderful red cable-stitch sweater and a skirt to match.

She could see Mamma's shoulders wearily bent over her sewing as she sat between the two work tables in their third-floor apartment and waited for the postman, hoping for a letter from her child.

Rosanne was afraid she had neglected far too many people since Yves had come into her life. She couldn't decide whether this was wicked of her, or just natural. But it did no good to brood. He was waiting for her downstairs and she was hurrying. That was what mattered.

Yves had settled himself in Uncle Henri's favorite armchair and the cat, Tempest, was in his lap. He looked completely at home. Colette was nowhere to be seen.

"Where is she?" Rosanne asked. "I thought she was with you."

"I thought she was with you."

"So there we are!"

Colette had vanished. Rosanne opened every door and shouted a childhood saying of theirs, "Wolf, are you there?" to make her laugh, but all in vain. Colette did not answer and they could not find her anywhere.

"She couldn't have gone out," Yves said. "I would have seen her. I haven't left the room."

Rosanne searched the house like a noisy weasel, even poking under the sofas, but no Colette.

"Let's go without her," whispered Yves, with such a coaxing smile that Rosanne started for the door. She wanted terribly to go, but Colette's disappearance began to worry her. Could she really have been asleep coming home from Haileybury that night, the memory of which sent shivers up and down Rosanne's spine, or had she just been pretending so as to spy on the two of them? Everything hung on the answer to that question.

Rosanne shouted till the echoes rang: "Colette! Colette!"

"What could have got into her?" the doctor grumbled, unaware of what might have caused Colette to run off.

"I guess she's had enough of chaperoning us," Rosanne said, knowing perfectly well what Colette had had enough of.

"Colette! Colette!"

Rosanne was just about to give up the evening out with Yves when she heard a sniffle behind her. Colette was in the kitchen clothes closet, her tear-stained face buried in an old felt hat. She looked up suspiciously and wiped her eyes on the printed scarf Uncle Bill had brought her from New York.

Rosanne tried to put her arms around her cousin, but Colette pushed her away roughly, crying, "Let me alone! Don't touch me!"

"But what's the matter with you? You were invited, too, for heaven's sake! What are you crying about? Did you think we'd leave you alone here? We hadn't the faintest intention . . ."

Rosanne's words were the essence of compassion. She could almost feel the angel wings sprouting from her shoulder blades, as she tried to quiet Colette. Not for anything, really, would she have left her cousin behind; she needed her too much for the sake of appearances.

"Oh, dear," thought Rosanne, ashamed of herself, "I don't dare break a single rule, and yet, here I am, trampling on Colette's heart with hobnailed boots just as if I were crunching gravel."

Somewhat embarrassed the doctor had gone outside to await the outcome of the conflict, ready, if necessary, to bandage the wounded participants. Colette was still crying, almost hysterical from the grief which, finally released after having been so long concealed, was overwhelming her. Rosanne kept insisting that she come along, and Colette argued that Rosanne was only trying to persuade her for purely selfish reasons.

"You should have stayed in Montréal," she sobbed. "Why did you come here to upset all our lives? We didn't need you. Oh, go away, leave me alone! Go kiss him in the dark some more!"

"So that's it, after all," said Rosanne quietly.

"I've had enough of you, and enough of Yves, and enough of chaperoning you two every single night. I'm never going with you again, never!"

But, finally, once she stopped crying, Colette dolefully allowed herself to be taken by the hand, as if she no longer had a will of her own, and went with them to the play.

When they returned home that night, she was ashamed of her anger and the spiteful words she had said to Rosanne, and cried on her shoulder as they lay in bed together, their arms around each other.

"Will you forgive me, Rosanne?"

It was Rosanne who should have asked Colette's pardon for dragging her into that gay auditorium, where her bleary eyes and swollen face were a bitter reproach to her cousin.

If Rosanne did not sink in the doctor's estimation that night, if she attached no importance to the callous, unthinking role he was playing, it was because neither of them saw very clearly how cruel their little game was.

"Of course, I forgive you, Colette," Rosanne said generously.

"What is my friendship worth after all? Not much," Rosanne felt. She gave an even more conclusive proof of that the next day, and it took Aunt Adèle to show her how wrong she had been.

"Do I have to be so selfish as to hurt people without caring?" Rosanne asked herself. She had once been so loving, so eager to please in order that every one would think well of her, and now being in love was rapidly destroying all her warmth and her common sense.

Colette had said nothing about the scene the night before, and Rosanne took good care not to mention it. She stayed behind while the others went to the bay, pretending she had to write some letters. She wanted to be alone because she was expecting a telephone call from Yves.

"Rosanne?" his deep voice said over the wire.

"Oh, is it you, Yves? How are you?" she replied casually. But "Oh, Yves, what a joy to hear you!" said her inner voice.

"Your Aunt Reine wants to go shopping in Rouyn, and she's asked me to drive her. It just happens I have a patient to see there, too. Say you'll come with us."

Rouyn! A hundred miles there, and a hundred back.

Two hundred miles with him! Still, Rosanne hesitated; "I don't know. Let me think it over a little."

"I'll give you one, two, three ticks of my watch, and then I'll demand a yes. You'll be spending the night at the hotel with your aunt, so bring what you'll need. I'll be along in just a few minutes, darling."

Darling! He had said "darling." She was his darling, *his,* his very own. She could scarcely catch her breath after that.

She held the receiver and stared at it as if she had never seen it before. *He* was determined she should go along. Her heart was pounding. She pressed her hand against her throat to keep from shouting her incredulous joy up and down Lake Street and through all of Ville-Marie.

Twenty minutes later she was waiting outside the house, suitcase in hand, her eyes shining. She had scribbled a note to Aunt Adèle: "Have gone to Rouyn with Aunt Reine and the doctor. Rosanne." After all, they certainly were being chaperoned, weren't they? So, there was obviously nothing for Aunt Adèle to worry about.

Later in the year, for some strange reason, Rosanne could not remember a single detail of the whole trip, only that it was one of the high moments of the summer. But she could recall all too vividly Aunt Adèle's attitude when she got back from Rouyn. Her aunt looked at her more severely than she ever had before—she who was usually so understanding and forgiving of her niece's whims, she who had really scolded Rosanne only once in all the five summers she had spent with the Vadeboncoeurs, and then, she had deserved it.

That had been when Rosanne was trying out Guy's new

air rifle. Clumsily, she had aimed it straight in front of her and hit the kitchen window. The BB-shot had grazed Aunt Adèle's head. Rosanne certainly had caught it then, but when her aunt had seen how sorry she was, she had softened up like a true mother.

"All right," she had said, "all's well that ends well. We won't say any more about it."

But this time Aunt Adèle was protecting her daughter's interests, and the justice of her cause made her firm. The face Rosanne met as she came in the door was not by any means the gentle one of Uncle Henri's dear Adèle.

"So, my fine young lady does not ask permission any more! She just goes off with the doctor without any notice whatsoever."

"But you weren't here, *Tante*. I left you a note."

Rosanne was arguing after a fashion, but the longer she confronted her aunt's unrelenting expression, the worse the situation became.

"I am responsible for you, Rosanne. Don't forget that. You should have waited till I got home."

"I couldn't. They would have gone without me. They were in a hurry."

Everything Rosanne said was putting her more in the wrong, as she was well aware. She was not used to scoldings, and she felt peculiar inside, as if she were shrinking, especially since she was clearly at fault.

"You didn't think," Aunt Adèle insisted sarcastically, "that Colette might have enjoyed a trip to Rouyn. Why didn't you suggest she come along?"

The answer was very simple. Rosanne had not thought of it at all, not for a second. But how could she say that to her aunt, or to Colette, who two nights before had so pitifully asked her pardon and who was listening, not two feet away, to her mother reprimanding Rosanne before the entire family.

As might have been expected, Rosanne burst into tears. Tense as a violin string, she fumbled in her pocket for a handkerchief she could not find. In her misery she dared to say, "I don't know why I didn't, *Tante*. I know I should have. I'm terribly sorry. If only you knew how sorry . . ."

"Your apologies are a little tardy, young lady. You have behaved very badly to Colette. How do you think I can continue to assume the responsibility I owe to your mother by having you here?"

Was she to be sent home on account of this foolish thing? She could not bear that now. She quickly thought of Aunt Reine. Every year she spent a week with her, and it was time she did so this summer. She would put the whole village between herself and the object of her remorse, Colette. Furthermore, she would be nearer Yves, since he lived in Aunt Reine's house.

"Aunt Adèle," Rosanne said, tears strangling her voice, "Aunt Reine has invited me to visit her. If you want me to, I'll go right now. I shall write Mamma tonight to explain . . ."

No more words would come. Rosanne went up to the bedroom she had shared with Colette, packed her bags, and came down. She was dismayed at the thought of having to face the hurt look in Uncle Henri's eyes; Colette, the cause of the whole scene; Marilou, who, of course, was taking her sister's part; and Aunt Adèle, who did not love her any more.

The living room was empty. Outside the door Henriette was waiting for her in the car.

"Come on," she said, taking Rosanne's suitcase. "I'll drive you. Don't take it so hard. The storm will blow over."

"What do you think of me?" Rosanne asked, incapable of seeing anything clearly and believing herself a permanent outcast.

"What do you want me to think, you little goose! You're in love with the doctor and it's as plain as day. In your situation anyone else would have done the same thing."

And so, Rosanne entered Castel Riant, the house of her grandmother, which was also the home of Aunt Reine, Uncle Sylvio and—Yves.

Chapter 12

Rosanne's grandfather had built his house out of solid pine, and it was spacious enough to have accommodated his eleven children. A few years after his death it had passed, by mutual agreement, into the capable hands of Uncle Sylvio and Aunt Reine, the true mistress of the establishment, who, like her mother, preserved the tradition of hospitality that was proverbial in the region. It was no small task, what with a family so social and so closely knit, who thought the truest joy in life was to share with others.

Like a fat mushroom Castel Riant squatted under a gray slate roof and faced the lake. It was a baronial mansion, and had been the most imposing house in the village until May's father, Horace Théroux, built one of brick, a rare thing in the Témiscamingue area.

Shaded by ancient maples, the house possessed a worn-out orchard in which the apples never grew larger than crab apples, a garden in which flourished giant rhubarb plants and hollyhocks, sweet peas that were the special care of Grandmamma, zinnias and phlox to decorate the church, and asparagus fern, which was considered indispensable to every bouquet. An ivy-covered fence surrounded this garden and screened the summerhouse that stood in the middle of it.

When its wide windows were open, it seemed as if one were actually outdoors. On the street side, a roofed balcony, on which pattering rain made a cheerful sound, gave the occupants a fabulous observation post. Thanks to its concealing screen of vines, Rosanne knew before anyone else did that banns had finally been posted for old Blaise Champagne and the woman he'd been courting for twenty years; that poor Germaine Bleau had fainted again at vespers; that Napoléon Lecavalier, the veterinary, had gone to confession twice on the same day. . . .

Grandmamma had reserved a large portion of the second floor for herself, and there she had her bedroom and her chapel. One never walked in on her unannounced, but instead tiptoed down the hall and, after knocking gently, entered her rooms sedately and properly.

All her grandchildren adored her, for she was intelligent and well-educated, a great lady to the tips of her toes, yet always approachable and without a trace of condescension in her manner. She was stout and had high color. In spite of her years, she carried herself very straight.

When her husband had left his profession of notary in the large town of Saint-Jérôme des Laurentides and had come to Témiscamingue with the first settlers in 1886, she had followed willingly.

"Why did you, Grandmamma?" Rosanne asked, wide-eyed, the first time they explored the past together. "What a funny thing to do, leave civilization for the wilderness."

"God has His plans for us, my child. Sometimes He chooses strange ways by which to show them to us. Three little white coffins. Three children taken from us in two days by a terrible epidemic of diphtheria. We were inconsolable."

"Did you want to start all over again to forget?"

"We were chiefly looking for some remedy for our despair. The best one is always hard work. Your grandfather had grown up on a farm. In spite of his university degree, he was devoted to the land. The spread of settlements seemed a lifesaver to us. Témiscamingue was virgin forest then, a new country where we could forget."

It was wonderful to have a grandmother who never tired of telling stories of her own past, which were more exciting than any one could read in books. That was how Rosanne learned that her grandparents, lured by the beautiful scenery and the fertile soil of the region, had moved north with their remaining two children, one girl of seven and another fourteen months old.

Ville-Marie had been called the Bay of the Fathers then. Five miles away were some Oblate missionaries, the only white men in the region except for a strange, bearded prospector, Hermit Kelly, who seldom strayed from his wretched hut.

"So I can say my grandfather founded Ville-Marie?"

"Yes, indeed, and you can be proud of it."

"Now I know why I love the village so. It's part of my inheritance. Really, Grandmamma, I could live here the rest of my life."

"Do you know how your grandfather happened to call it Ville-Marie?"

"I haven't the faintest idea. Isn't it the name Montréal once had, way back when it was founded in the seventeenth century?"

"Yes, and soon after our arrival we wanted to baptize the bay that, but it took us a long time to do it."

"Is Ville-Marie in honor of the Blessed Virgin Mary?"

"Of course. Your grandfather petitioned the authorities, who replied that it was ridiculous to pick a name already identified with Montréal and refused him permission. But they didn't know how persistent my Elzéar could be. He patiently bided his time. A few years later the first County Assembly, of which he was a member, gave Ville-Marie its present name."

What impressed Rosanne most was the trip through the wilderness in open wagon and canoe. In those days the railroad ended at Mattawa, about a hundred miles from her grandparents' destination.

"You were on your own, with a hundred miles to go?" Rosanne asked.

"Through forests and rivers and lakes," her grandmother replied. "The only vehicle that could get through the bogs around the Érables Rapids was a cart drawn by two horses so old and weak they really belonged on the wagon instead of in the shafts. Then, we had to cross the Ottawa River on a raft. The water was choked with logs and we were sure our raft would be rammed. It was getting very dark and the children were terribly hungry and tired."

Rosanne, who was none too brave, imagined what her fears would have been had she been lost in the hostile darkness of the bush. As she pictured the scene, she remembered something. "Grandmamma, weren't you expecting a baby at the time?"

Grandmamma laughed. "Yes, your poor Uncle Alphonse. But in spite of the rough journey I took before his birth, I've never seen a more beautiful child than that one. Hardships forge healthy bodies and strong minds."

At Long-Sault, they had to cross Lake Témiscamingue against a strong wind and against the current in a birchbark canoe. Then, after a three-mile portage, they came to a house where they found shelter for the night. They were not home yet. It took a whole day to cross the last bay in their tiny canoe, and they landed at midnight before a rude cabin which had been put together by loggers at Grandpapa's request.

"Midnight?" inquired Rosanne. "Why midnight?"

"We didn't mean to dramatize, dear, but we couldn't make it in daylight because of the wind. You know how large our bay is. The cabin was a haven to us; we were so exhausted. But how crude it was! The partitions inside were of unbleached muslin and the window frames were covered with gray wool blankets, for there were no window panes. In one of the rooms, enough cut wood was piled to see us through the winter. Our baggage and furniture, which was supposed to follow from Mattawa, took three months to catch up with us. Your grandfather had to turn cabinet-maker, and with his own hands made the most necessary pieces."

With two workhorses Grandfather cleared his land. Two loggers, the Miron brothers, helped him to build his first real house, and shortly afterward Grandfather opened a general store to meet the needs of the settlers.

In the fall of that same year a son was born to Grand-mamma, the first white child in Témiscamingue. Uncle Alphonse got used to being sat on, for his cradle did not arrive till a week after the stork did, and his temporary bed was the only armchair, but still he seemed to thrive.

The first Mass of the village was sung in the new house, and Grandfather's integrity and courage began to be rec-ognized. He was elected to all sorts of positions: Land Agent for the Crown, Clerk of the Circuit Court, Mayor of Ville-Marie, County Magistrate. Yet in spite of these official duties, he still conducted his own notary business.

Grandmamma was just the kind of wife such a man needed, Rosanne felt. Friendly with everyone, she was as much at ease with a poor woman who came begging at the door as with a Senator's wife. Rosanne loved the old lady with all her heart because of what she had done, and because of the kindness she lavished upon her grandchildren and children.

Since the death of her husband she had worn only black, but she was interested in everyone, and she tried so hard to keep up with the times that she became almost a modern woman. Then, after two of her daughters became nuns, she turned more and more to her religion. As the years passed, she continued her voluntary withdrawal from the world, for in it she found the strength of peace. How she could laugh and tease and make fun of one, though! She was a tireless letter-writer, with the widest correspondence of anyone in the district. And such a rapid and skillful darner of socks that the whole family brought theirs to her to be mended.

Rosanne never wearied of being with her, and she loved to be invited upstairs to the regal apartment where her grandmother's many souvenirs—photographs, old letters, prayerbooks, curios—lived in the dignity they deserved. Rosanne quickly confessed her affection for the doctor, since she knew that her grandmother thought highly of him. But, like Aunt Adèle, Grandmamma, too, advised Rosanne to be careful.

"He's a ladies' man, so be on your guard."

"Oh, nonsense, Grandmamma, a girl is always sure of how a man feels about her. He's interested in me, to say the least."

"I don't deny it. He has eyes only for you. He laughs at all your jokes, even the poor ones, and they've been getting worse and worse for quite some time now. You may think he's all yours. But will it last? Wait a bit, dear child."

When Grandmamma said "Wait a bit" like that, Rosanne couldn't help thinking of one of the most touching experiences in her grandmother's life: the return to Canada of her eldest daughter. Adrienne had been a Franciscan missionary in the Philippines, where she had contracted a disease that could not be cured. Her superiors had thought it best to send her back to their Québec monastery.

Grandmother had hurried to the provincial capital to meet her, to take her in her arms once more, to rub out every memory of their separation. When she got to the reception room of the convent she could hardly keep from running straight into the cloister, so great was her impatience to see her daughter. But when Adrienne finally appeared, wearing the same calm smile as always, Grandmamma, instead of rushing up to her, just sat and held her by the hand.

"Wait a bit," she said. "The joy is too great. Wait a bit, dear child."

Wait, think it over, study and consider and deliberate before acting—that was, Rosanne thought, the secret of her grandmother's wisdom. She must have owed much of her remarkable dignity to that self-discipline. Rosanne envied her, but she did not try to emulate her. From now on, she did not intend to wait to have her joy; she wanted it right away.

Every morning of her stay at Castel Riant she went up the big staircase at the end of the hall, which was as wide as three of the rooms in Rosanne's Montréal home put together, to Grandmamma's apartment. Every time, she patted the bronze goddess with the lamp that stood on the newel post. Once upstairs, she listened to another story that always seemed new, told in that old, sweet voice.

Aunt Reine had given the doctor a large room on the

second floor with a view of the bay. Rosanne used to rummage around in it when he was out, sniffing the scent of his tobacco, fingering his possessions. She always finished with a look at the photograph of his mother that stood on his chest of drawers. How would Madame Renaud like her? she often wondered.

Rosanne herself had the guest room on the first floor. In Uncle Sylvio's office she had come upon a framed photograph of the doctor with other important men of the village. She used to sneak in like a burglar to gaze at his face, which stood out clearly in the front row. She would examine every feature: his straight nose, his hair which was as black as Uncle René's but more plentiful; his sad smile, and his eyes.

One evening Aunt Reine caught Rosanne coming out of the empty office.

"Well," she said, "what are you up to in there?"

Hoping that no one knew why she went there so often, Rosanne answered, blushing, "I was looking something up in the encyclopedia."

Yves, of course, spent most of his time in his office. They had breakfast together, he in his gray jacket that never seemed to wear out, and Rosanne in her prettiest housecoat, to the distress of her grandmother, who would have liked to see her a little more conventional in costume and behavior. At last Rosanne was herself, away from Colette, whom she had not seen again, and far from Aunt Adèle. Yves, too, was now free from restraint. His manner toward Rosanne was of playful gentleness, but in return she would raise her little wall of resistance.

Near the end of her visit, the wall collapsed all at once. They were coming home from a game of tennis in which Yves had beaten her soundly as usual.

"It's nice and cool in here," he said as they entered the living room, where the shades had been drawn against the stifling midday heat. "Go sit down, Rosanne, and I'll fix you a lemonade."

He leaned over her, looking into her eyes and smiling. Suddenly something flashed between them, something so dizzily exciting that they were irresistibly drawn together. His lips pressed against hers.

"Pretty Rosanne," he said.

Rosanne was blushing. She wanted to leap up and run away so that she could savor the moment properly, but she also wanted him to keep kissing her. Before she could decide which would be better, Yves decided for her.

"The lemonade!" he said suddenly. "I forgot the lemonade."

He left her there, her face blushing furiously as Aunt Reine came into the living room, her knitting bag under one arm.

"Why, Rosanne, how red in the face you are!" she said. "Are you alone? Where's Yves?"

"In the kitchen. He's fixing a lemonade."

"And how your eyes are shining! Has something been going on?"

It was so obvious that Rosanne thought she might as well confess.

"He kissed me, *Tante*."

"On the mouth? He kissed you on the mouth?"

"Yes."

Aunt Reine did not seem to know whether she should be shocked or amused. "Well, it looks as if you've made a conquest."

"Oh, yes!"

"He kissed me," Rosanne kept saying over and over to herself the rest of the afternoon, as if she would never tire of the words. "He loves me. He loves me!"

Chapter 13

THAT SAME EVENING, over the fruit and cheese at supper, Yves suddenly announced, "I should like my mother to know Rosanne. I'm sure they would get on well together."

Rosanne smiled demurely, as she felt a proper young girl should, but she was really impatient to try her strength against the original of the photograph in Yves' room, her mother-in-law-to-be.

Grandmamma seemed quite pleased with this important announcement, and Aunt Reine, a loyal ally since the little episode that morning, suggested with her usual generosity, "Why don't you ask her to come and spend a few days with us here? I should be delighted to have her, Yves, and we can keep Rosanne a little longer."

"I'm afraid the trip would be too much for her. Mamma is getting old, and it's a long way from here to the Gaspé peninsula where she lives. But my vacation is about due, and I thought I might take Rosanne to our house in Percé if she would like to go."

Rosanne wanted to very much, and she said so for all to hear. Her wall of defense against showing him how much in love she was had been stormed, and was crumbling into ruins. Now, whenever Yves looked at her, she was defenseless. As the days passed, she literally radiated happiness.

"Rosanne is growing very attractive," remarked Uncle Sylvio, who was quite a connoisseur of pretty girls. "See how her eyes sparkle and how pink her cheeks are."

Rosanne smiled. She loved Yves; he loved her; the world was perfect. He loved her? Did he really? She was assured of it; it was no longer a mere hope. He had said so in the time-honored words she was expecting.

They had been sitting in his car before the house, and he had been telling her about his family, his home, his village, when suddenly he asked bluntly, "Do you love me, Rosanne?"

"Why does he have to ask?" she thought. "He knows perfectly well I love him." She was in such confusion she could only whisper, "Yes."

Her head was resting on the back of the seat. He brought his face close to hers.

"You said 'yes' as if you were signing your own death warrant," he said. "Look at me, *petite* rose."

"No, not right away. Give me time to collect my thoughts."

"How involved you girls make things. You, especially.

What in the world are you scowling so for? Are you sorry you love me?"

"No, no, no, no! Just the opposite. It's a wonderful feeling."

"Then why such a mournful expression?"

"I don't know. I'm afraid, I guess. The feeling is too complicated for me."

"You're a sweet little thing. So intense!"

"That's the word I was looking for—intense. It's the intensity of the feeling that frightens me. It's made me do things I hardly understand, and then . . . and then . . ."

"And then what? Don't be scared; tell me. Then what?"

"You haven't told me if you . . ."

He laughed, and drew her to him, murmuring so softly that she felt rather than heard his answer.

"Yes, you darling little fool, I do. I do love you."

Suddenly there was someone pounding down the street.

"Doctor! Doctor!" a voice shouted. "Come to the pier quick! A girl has drowned! They're trying to find her. Hurry!"

A crowd of people was running toward the pier. Rosanne and Yves had been so absorbed that they had been oblivious to the confusion around them.

"A girl," thought Rosanne, terrified. "Could it be Colette?" Her imagination took a fearful leap and pictured her unhappy, neglected cousin driven to some desperate act.

She tore herself away from Yves' arms and leaped from the car, crying, "Oh, Lord, it can't be Colette. She wouldn't."

It was growing dusk. A woman leaned over the edge of the wharf, peering into the rough water.

"It's the Widow Doré," someone told Rosanne, who nearly fainted with relief. "Her only child was playing by the edge and fell in."

Some boys had stripped off their clothes and were diving off a nearby barge in a frantic effort to locate the body.

As the darkness closed in, they recovered the little girl. Yves tried to restore life to her stiffened limbs, by administering artificial respiration. He refused to let anyone spell him for fear of interrupting the rhythm. Finally, he had to stop before he himself succumbed to exhaustion.

Then, at last, all hope gone, neighbors of Widow Doré carried the child away. The bystanders scattered, some going home with the distraught mother, others spreading the story of the accident as they paused at every doorstep they passed, rendering it more dramatically each time.

Rosanne and Yves stayed on the pier, the only ones left. The lake reflected the crescent moon as beautifully as ever. The whole landscape was bathed in a silvery light rather like the fabric of a dream.

Yves was very tired, and deeply distressed that all his efforts had failed. As he leaned against a pile, he kept looking up at the stars, appearing one by one in the black sky. Yet he did not seem to see them, and though his lips were moving, no sound came from them. At last she had found a way by which she might become a part of his life. He needed her to fight by his side in his daily battle against sickness and hurt; needed her to console him in his despair when he lost. A shoulder to lean upon, a heart that would respond. She was sure she could be all that to him—his joy, his strength, his rest.

She laid her hand gently on his shoulder, her first spontaneous gesture of love to him.

"Come, Yves," she said. "Come, we must go home."

"Better to be a logger or a plowman," he said despairingly. "The trees and the earth don't reproach you. But to see the look in the eyes of a parent when . . . Let's get out of here, Rosanne. Let's go just as far as we can. Oh, if you only knew how I long for a vacation, for just a little rest."

Rosanne's role, compounded of gentleness and sympathy, was greatly pleasing to her. The breeze was ruffling his hair. She stroked it and murmured words of comfort. Raising his face toward her, he asked a totally unexpected question that emanated, she supposed, out of some half-formed ideas in his mind.

"Rosanne, do you think two people can live comfortably on five thousand dollars a year?"

"Aha," she crowed to herself, "that sounds very much like a proposal of marriage!" She did not know what to answer, and her pride kept her from shouting "yes" as she really wished to do. She was torn between the desire to exclaim, "Darling, I would live with you in a hut, if I had to," and her fear of seeming too forward.

"I should think so, yes," she said hesitantly, as if she weren't too sure. "Mamma gets along on less than that, and there are four of us, my two brothers, her, and myself, at home. But it's no fortune, of course."

Then it was too late; she realized the mistake she had made. "Oh, you clumsy, proud little fool!" she thought.

She should have kissed him and convinced him that she could do it easily. But that would have been too bold, openly indicating that she was waiting, with a "yes" ready on her tongue, for him to blurt out the question. She didn't dare. So, instead, she had been stupidly noncommittal. "What if it weren't a fortune? Money did not matter at all. Only his love did." She had completely spoiled her chances. Yves said no more, and took her back to the house. It was all she deserved, she cried to herself.

Two letters were waiting on the hall table, one for Yves from Percé, and one for Rosanne from Montréal.

"Mamma wants to know when I am taking my vacation. She is inviting you to come home with me," Yves told her. "What does yours say?"

Rosanne had written home to ask whether or not she could go.

"Permission granted——"

"Wonderful!"

"——on condition that a reliable person goes with us on the trip. 'Reliable' is heavily underscored."

Both of them laughed at the thought that now they had to turn up a "reliable" person. Uncle Sylvio was in the living room, playing his favorite waltz on the phonograph. Yves grabbed Rosanne in his arms and enthusiastically whirled her around the chairs and tables in time to the music.

For the next two days they did nothing but talk about

who the reliable person would be. Someone jokingly suggested old Baptiste, or Father Hébert. Finally it was decided, somewhat against Rosanne's wishes, that Eve should go with them.

Rosanne had no great love for Eve, even though she was her cousin quite as much as Colette. She did not like the boldness of Eve's ways, her loud giggle, her short skirts, her slang, or the careless way she spoke to her parents and relatives. Besides, she was far too pretty. She batted her long eyelashes like a movie actress, and yet she was not quite fifteen years old. "What," Rosanne thought, "will Eve be like when she is twenty, for heaven's sake!"

Since she was the only person available, and since Yves said he was pleased with that arrangement, there was nothing for Rosanne to do but agree. She consented to Eve's driving with them to Percé with a stopover in Montréal.

The night before they left, Aunt Adèle came to say good-by and to bring Rosanne some fudge.

"We'll be waiting for you when you come back, Rosanne."

"How sweet of you, *Tante.*"

"Colette hopes, too, that you will forgive our attitude. She did not dare come to kiss you good-by. But she really wants to."

"Where is she?"

"In the summerhouse."

Rosanne ran outside and into Colette's arms. They were laughing and crying all at once.

"Rosanne!"

"Colette, dear Colette, you aren't angry with me any more?"

"Not so much, anyway. I'll tell you why when you come back. I've come to a wonderful decision, and I'll tell you about that, too. So hurry back!"

"You're making my mouth water. Tell me now!"

"No, not till you come back."

"I'll die of curiosity."

"Then you'll just have to."

So Rosanne and Colette parted friends and summer sisters once more. Aunt Adèle had forgiven Rosanne. She was leaving on the trip with Yves. "Life couldn't be more beautiful," she thought, "and yet . . ."

Chapter 14

WHEN THEY LEFT the next morning, the sun was shining warm and bright over the fields. Yves was in high spirits and Rosanne pretended to be completely indifferent to Eve, who flirted pertly with the doctor on every possible occasion. Eve wore a new light blue dress that flattered her china-doll complexion and her well-brushed blond hair which hung in a pony tail to her waist. "How pretty she is," Rosanne was forced to admit, "a little charmer, with her wide, innocent eyes and her carefully shaped eyebrows."

They had not gone a hundred miles before Rosanne had had quite enough of her and her New York. "In New York, you see . . ." She talked about it incessantly. It had the tallest buildings, the greatest population, the most beautiful sights. Rosanne would a thousand times rather have gone to New York herself, even if she had to walk on her hands, than listen to Eve's travelogue. But Yves was amused by her chatter—jabber, Rosanne would have called it.

When they stopped at restaurants, young men looked enviously at Yves, accompanied by two attractive girls. Eve grinned back at them, displaying her even white teeth. Rosanne assumed a well-brought-up-young-lady expression, both to discourage enterprising young men and to rebuke the shameless Eve.

"Eve, what are you thinking of? Behave yourself, for heaven's sake!" Rosanne said.

Eve shrugged. "Really, Roz, let me have a little fun. Don't be so old-fashioned."

"I old-fashioned?" thought Rosanne. Well, she certainly was aging every minute she had to watch Eve's performance in the confines of the car and listen to her silly talk, which for some strange reason, seemed to charm Yves.

Every time they stopped, there was a struggle to see who would get the seat next to the driver. Eve made a dash for it, and so did Rosanne. They would get to the door at the same instant, and then shove each other with their shoulders, elbows and hips, all the time clinging for dear life to the car door, until finally Rosanne's superior strength won out. She was ashamed of these squabbles. They were like two children after the same toy.

Yves remained indifferent to these hostilities, the strategy of which seemed to escape him. Now that he was on vacation, he smiled so often that sometimes Rosanne wished he would resume his usual solemn expression just to prove he was capable of some serious thoughts.

Underneath her pretended disinterest, Rosanne grew increasingly uneasy. She had been counting on this trip to introduce a handsome and respectable fiancé to Mamma and her brothers. But the way things were going, Eve would have won out over her before they got to Percé.

When they reached Montréal, Rosanne felt that circumstances conspired against her in a way that was almost laughable. They were no sooner at the Fontaines' exchanging cordial greetings, than Mamma took out of her pocket a telegram for Yves.

He read it hurriedly and handed it to Rosanne. His young sister had been injured in an accident, and had been taken to a hospital in Québec, where his mother was waiting for him. She begged him to come there as soon as he could, and apologized to Rosanne for this unfortunate change in plans.

"You'll go alone, of course," said Mamma, who hastened to sympathize with him.

"There goes la Gaspésie," Eve sulked.

"Will you excuse us?" Rosanne said, making it clear that she wanted to be alone with Yves.

Mamma took Eve into the kitchen, where Rosanne's two young brothers, Fabien and Simon, surveyed her from top to toe and whistled with admiration.

Rosanne was seeing her home clearly for the first time, for she was seeing it through the eyes of another: Yves. After the comfortable houses of her aunts, how bare it seemed, how much the home of a poor relation, in spite of its brave efforts at dignity. The shabby upholstery, the chipped ornaments, the dingy plaster on the ceiling, the old-fashioned furniture were hateful to Rosanne. Mamma's lovely dress, the company manners of the two boys could not hide the fact that here a widow and her children lived a penny-pinching life.

Rosanne was ashamed. She was viewing things and people in a new and painfully realistic perspective. She was astonished at the way they appeared now. Eve became superficial and selfish; Yves, a little worn like the chairs, smaller in stature, and insincere; and Mamma . . . With eyes wide open at last Rosanne saw the careworn face, the stooped shoulders, the dark-circled eyes, the thin cheeks. Suddenly she loved her mother so much she forgot the man beside her. Mamma had sewed and sewed to earn her a summer of vacation, and she had been wickedly ungrateful. She was about to go off and leave her in order to marry this stranger whom, for a fleeting moment, she savagely hated for having come between them.

She wondered what was going on behind the deep wrinkles in Yves' stubborn forehead. What was he thinking as he sat in the best armchair in the workroom and took in the details of the apartment—the cracked window patched with adhesive tape, the clean square on the wall where a picture had been taken down, and the fat brown cockroach that crept out of the woodwork to go unconcernedly about its business.

He had not said a word, apparently crushed by the news of his sister's accident and the way his vacation plans had been disrupted. Now he would not have the sunshine and the rest and the long days with Rosanne and Eve he had hoped for. Rosanne pitied him, but she did not tell him so, for she was held back by her new sense of loyalty toward her family.

"I'm leaving right away. How upset you must be with me, Rosanne."

"I am terribly disappointed, Yves. The idea was probably too lovely to work."

"What will become of Eve?"

"How concerned he is about her," Rosanne thought bitterly. Then aloud she said, "She can stay here. You can pick us both up on your way back. Don't worry about us, and let me hear from you just as soon as possible."

All her plans had tumbled down like a house of cards. Now she would have to go out with that spiteful Eve in a city at which the girl turned up her nose. Fortunately there was Mamma, to whom Rosanne told everything little by little. One day, suddenly, Mrs. Fontaine put into words what her daughter had been trying not to think about, "I did not know that Eve was so pretty. You aren't afraid the doctor . . . ?"

Rosanne not only was afraid, she was sure of it. Since Yves left, she had not had a single word from him, yet he was the same man who just a week before had told her he loved her and called her his darling.

Ever since his departure, she had waited for the postman like a woman whose husband is at war. Every day, at the same hour, she would greet him as if he had not been to the apartment for days; and every day he would go away, leaving her with nothing but worry and a bad temper.

Yves wrote no more often than he spoke. Rosanne could imagine the day when the postman would be so flattered by her attentions that he would invite her to a band concert in Lafontaine Park. And then, when she had almost stopped hoping, she got the letter she had been waiting for so long.

Three sentences. His sister was getting well. His mother and he were going back to Percé. It had rained. "Sincerely, Yves R." "Sincerely! Why not 'Very truly yours,' while he was at it?" Rosanne asked herself. She carefully hid the letter away. It proved Mamma had been right in her suspicions. Surely, one doesn't write that kind of letter to a woman one really loves. "Sincerely!" Who wanted his sincerity? Rosanne was burning with impatience to learn the reason for his change in attitude, but nothing would alter her decision to go back to Ville-Marie at any cost.

"Don't get so upset, Rosanne," Mamma pleaded. "You're not sure he's deceived you. If he loves you, he will come back to you. Don't jump to conclusions. You are so young. You have all your life ahead of you."

"I love him, Mamma." She could think of no other words to explain the turmoil of her feelings. "The rest doesn't matter. I love him. Can't you understand?"

"Why not?"

Mamma was smiling. She, too, had once been that much in love. "Mamma in love!" Rosanne could not get over her astonishment.

When Yves' two weeks of vacation were ove
up unexpectedly at the end of a terribly hot aft
sanne was coming back from the hairdresse
rumpled and her hair curled tight to her scal
permanent wave. Eve, just out of one of her s
her skin as fresh as a rose petal, threw her arms
and kissed him eagerly on the mouth.

"Oh, at last you're here!" she exclaimed, a
not bear to remain with Rosanne's family anot

Yves was going to prolong their embra
caught sight of Rosanne at the turn in the stair
and freed himself from Eve's plump arms.

"Hello, Rosanne."

That was all. It was a bone tossed to a
Rosanne." She shivered, even though it was
the shade.

"I'm leaving tomorrow," he said. "Who
me?"

"I am, I am," Eve caroled.

"I am, too," Rosanne said in a somewhat l

Mamma tried to keep Rosanne from reti
Marie but failed. Rosanne felt her happiness
and she was determined to stay with him,
unexpected coolness.

"Your mother seems to suffer from the
as they went down to his car, leaving Mrs. F
good-by as cheerily as she could. "You shou
her, Rosanne. She's worn out with work."

"What do you mean, Doctor?" She had not dared call him by his first name since he had become so cold and distant.

"I am not saying this idly, Rosanne. You should realize that your mother is working too hard. She needs you to help her."

Rosanne could have cried. He was blaming her for leaving Mamma. Or was that his way of saying he did not want her company? He seemed very ill at ease with her; his shoulder stiffened whenever she touched it, and he hardly ever looked at her.

Having suggested that she should have remained in Montréal, thus warning her subtly that his interest in her was waning and that it was time for a fresher love, his duty had been done; he felt free to steal glances at Eve over Rosanne's lowered head.

At the first stopping place, he took Eve by the hand and repeated words he had used before, "You get in first, Eve. Sit next to me."

That was the last straw. "Oh, Colette, you are well avenged," brooded Rosanne. Well avenged, too, would be all the country belles Yves had spurned for her. With a little patience they would have their turn also in his fickle heart, so patently free to all.

"Enjoy your triumph, Eve," she thought as she watched her rub against him like a kitten. "It will be as short as it is dazzling."

The return trip was a fiasco. It rained every mile, turning the dusty summer roads into muddy tracks. Yves was

sick at his stomach and got hives after Eve argued him into eating a strawberry tart.

Rosanne was in a hurry to get to Ville-Marie, and at the same time she dreaded arriving. Soon everyone would know the story. The village people, the aunts, the friends, all those who had prophesied an engagement and expected her to return with a ring, would have a good laugh at her, another victim of the doctor's summer love.

Rosanne's first romance was finished, good and finished. She knew that now. Yves would never again call her his darling; his hand would never grope for hers, or his lips touch her lips. "What a dreary thing the rest of the summer will be," she lamented, "with my dream in ashes at my feet." There was no way for her to go home alone; she would just have to wait and suffer, seeing Eve and the doctor together until the Vadeboncoeurs were ready to leave Ville-Marie for their autumn trip to the city.

Shoved over against the window, on which the rain was beating ceaselessly, Rosanne felt thoroughly wretched. Her misery was like a great lump inside her. In her low voice Eve was singing an old love song Marilou had taught her. It spoke to Rosanne about things now gone—Yves' infrequent laugh, his one gray jacket, his easy victories at tennis, the expression that came into his eyes when he was moved.

"Who are you singing that song for, Eve?" Yves asked casually.

Rosanne could have screamed.

"For you, Yves. Who else?" Eve murmured.

She had him completely in the palm of her clinging little hand. "Well, let her play with him," gloated Rosanne.

"Let him suffer, the way he made us—Colette and me—suffer."

Rosanne understood perfectly now why Colette had rebelled that night the three of them were to go to the theater. There had been nothing else for her to do; now Rosanne almost approved of her defiance. Never before had her cousin been so dear to her. It was to Colette she would run in her distress. To her she could say what she did not dare say to herself: "Colette, he doesn't love me any more."

And her cousin would be sweet and sympathetic, though there might be a trace of a smile on her mouth, as she replied, "My poor baby, I knew it."

*

Chapter 15

Rosanne returned to Ville-Marie disillusioned and heartbroken. Eve had spoiled everything. Probably by next Christmas some other young thing would put Eve out of the running, and by the year after, still another pretty unsuspecting girl would be substituted. That thought, however, relieved Rosanne of none of her pain. In losing Yves, she had also lost her dream of a life in Ville-Marie and many of her illusions about herself. Poems, songs, nature itself just reopened the wound. "Why," she wondered, "should it be such fine weather when I am feeling so miserable?"

Grandmamma tried hard to convince her it was all for the best, and that she would come to see this episode in her life as a valuable experience.

"Look realities in the face," she said, when Rosanne went to cry on her shoulder. "It's time you came out of your dream world. It is not a man you loved, it's the village he lived in, that little corner of the earth where you were born, with its blue sky and its lake breezes. Don't you see, Rosanne, dear, that in loving our fickle little doctor you were only loving yourself?"

"Grandmamma!" Rosanne was shocked.

"Yes, I mean it. He was only your notion of what happiness is. For a girl of sixteen like you, such a dream romance is perfectly normal, as a matter of fact."

"But I keep telling you it was solid, real. I wanted to help him, share his work, dedicate myself to his happiness. I never thought of myself for a single minute."

"Not consciously, perhaps. And you were sincere, I have no doubt. Otherwise you wouldn't have that poor, sad little face. You are too young, also. How can anyone think . . ."

Grandmamma broke off, slightly embarrassed at recalling that she had been married at sixteen. Then she went on more forcefully than ever, "If your romance had ended in marriage, I would have been glad. One can easily learn by oneself how to live with joy; but with pain it is more difficult. So, understand while you are still young that a little suffering is necessary to build a strong character."

"Mine *is* strong, Grandmamma. But I shall never get over Yves."

"Never is a big word. Time is a great healer, believe me."

But Rosanne clung to her troubles.

"Everything was so fine and lovely and wonderful. And then, bang! Nothing but having to watch him and that simpering Eve. Why, Grandmamma? I prayed. If God is good, why does He allow His creatures to suffer so terribly?"

Grandmamma laughed. When she could catch her breath again, she said, "Suffer! Oh, my dear child. You refuse to bow to fate. You haven't exhausted all your rebelliousness yet. Do you know whom you remind me of?" She stroked Rosanne's hair. "You make me think of Job."

"That's a funny thing to say. Why Job?"

"Because he also asked the Lord, 'Why?' He said, 'Behold, I cry out of wrong, but I am not heard: I cry aloud, but there is no judgment. . . . He hath destroyed me on every side.'"

"The poor man was right. But how did God answer Job? What could He say to justify Himself?"

Grandmamma took her Bible from her desk and thumbed through the yellow pages, amused at the way she had calmed her granddaughter. Slowly she read from the book of Job, "'Who is this that darkeneth counsel by words without knowledge, He answered out of the whirlwind. Then Job humbled himself, therefore have I uttered that I understood not; things too wonderful for me that I knew not.'"

"So I, too, have been talking through my hat?"

"Yes."

"But, good heavens, it's my life. It seems to me I have a right to talk about it."

"You have your place in God's plan, even you, just the same as Job, and as your mother, and as I. Did you think it was easy for me to see my children die? Or that your mother was not grief-stricken when your father was killed in that dreadful accident? Still, we learned to smile again. So, you, too, will forget."

"It would be easier if Yves were dead."

"That's your wounded pride talking. That's what is making you say these foolish things."

Grandmamma was telling the truth. Exasperated by her frankness, Rosanne took the big leather-bound Bible out of her hands. In the complaint of Job she found words to express her misery and explain it to her grandmother who, she felt, did not want to understand. " 'The days of affliction have taken hold upon me. . . . When I waited for light, there came darkness. . . . I went mourning without the sun,' " she read as she flipped the pages of the familiar book.

Grandmamma shook her head, looking for more concrete arguments. And, as always, she found them.

"When I told you of our hardships as pioneers," she said, as if she were entrusting Rosanne with a confidence, "I did not tell you the worst. Did it ever occur to you, Rosanne, that I gave birth to your uncle Alphonse in the depths of the wilderness?"

"Was it so very bad?"

"I am not talking about the physical pain. I expected that, and welcomed it, for I knew what it meant. No, the worst was the repugnance I had to conquer. My midwife was a dirty old savage. I shuddered every time he touched me with his gnarled hands, but then I would set my teeth and throw myself on the mercy of Providence. Then the child was born, healthy and lovely. The old Indian laid him on the bed near me, and he smiled at me for the first time. 'You good,' he said. 'You brave. You bring good luck to your papoose.'"

Grandmamma picked up the counterpane and threw it over her shoulders Indian fashion, and stuck her quill pen in her chignon. "Rosanne, you good! You brave! You bring good luck to your future wigwam."

Rosanne laughed at the mimicry in spite of herself. Then her grandmother grew serious.

"You will be all the stronger for having been deceived, my darling. I am sure that you have enough poise to find a way to be happy, no matter where you are. Do you know why?"

"Why?"

"Because there is something in you that is always seeking perfection itself. Someday a man will come along whom you will truly love, not for yourself but for himself, not as you loved this one who wasn't worth the trouble and who didn't care. Then, my child, you won't have to put up with this nonsense from your old grandmother."

"So all this agony I've been going through from morning till night won't have been for nothing?"

"No suffering is for nothing. You think you are small and feeble and hurt, but I see you already as the woman you will be someday, partly because you have had a great disappointment now."

"What a relief it is," thought Rosanne, "to have a grandmother to talk to this frankly, who scolds you and teases you with such loving persistence."

Before saying good-by, her grandmother slipped a five-dollar bill into Rosanne's hand and said in a conspiratorial way, "For something foolish."

Rosanne left, feeling much happier. She breathed in great gulps of the lake air. Her feet were moving as if in time to a march. Already her self-assurance was beginning to reassert itself. Then, she looked up and saw Yves' car going down the road; he was taking Eve for a drive in the country. Her good resolutions had to be put off until another day.

Rosanne had nothing to remember him by, not a photograph or a gift or a love letter other than the curt note in Montréal. She had nothing but memories to cry over. But she could play the game of indifference, too. He would never know the place he had held, and still held, in her life, nor the pain he had caused her. If she played her game well, everyone would think they had parted by mutual consent. Rosanne would avoid him as if she had discovered some fault in him, some fault it was impossible for her to overlook. Her pride would be saved. And even if she only fooled herself, at least she would forget her despair.

In spite of all these proud decisions, she wandered the length of Main Street looking for him. There was his drugstore beside the post office and opposite Uncle René's general store. Uncle René must have wondered what was wrong with his niece. She had seldom visited his store before. Now, she went to see him daily under the pretext of doing an errand. She hid behind the counters and watched Yves' goings and comings through the shop window. If Yves went to the post office, she rushed over there to buy stamps. By the end of the summer, she could have stamped the Christmas cards of her entire family with the collection she accumulated.

While in the post office, she read the local paper, and from behind her barricade of folded pages she would glare at him. He tried to greet her, but she turned up her nose. Then as she passed by, she haughtily pushed him aside with her shoulder.

When Rosanne told Colette what brave things she did, Colette laughed at finding her cousin so like herself.

"Look, *mon chou,*" she said, "when I saw the sly doctor with our dear cousin Eve the night before you went to Montréal, I knew right away that we were going to be friends again."

"Did you see it happening even then?"

"Yes, it was then that I wiped out all your—well—let's say your blunders, and swore to myself that I would rescue you from moping if I had to pull you out by the scruff of your neck. Can't you imagine his triumph if he were to see us on all the sidewalks and street corners weeping over having lost him?"

Then an unexpected and small thing happened which changed Rosanne's attitude. One day ten of the cousins were picking blueberries on the side of the mountain. They scattered in their search for more bushes and Rosanne was left alone on a ledge that overlooked the valley. The lake glistened below her and lapped at the base of the cliff. She stretched out in the shade of a tree, her arms folded under her head, and gazed up at the sky flecked with drifting clouds.

The scent of pine needles filled the air. The wind was

ruffling her hair. A bird lit on the bush, fearlessly stared right into her eyes, and then burst into song. It seemed to her to be in praise of the joy of living, and the fine sunny day, and the part he played in the whole scheme of things.

Her bitterness and hurt dropped from her like a cloak no longer needed. She went down the mountainside at peace with herself and no longer angry at not having what she had wanted. Colette caught up with her and they walked hand in hand, smiling at each other. They were free of the doctor; there would be no more dreams when they saw his face. Rosanne would return to her mother, whom she missed terribly; and Colette, with her parents' approval, was to enroll as a student nurse at Sainte-Justine, Montréal's hospital for French children. Rosanne would help her mother and her brothers; Colette would care for sick boys and girls. The happiness they no longer expected from Yves they would find elsewhere.

So the enchanted summer drew to a close. Rosanne surveyed the street she loved so much, saying good-by to every house, every hedge, every clump of seed-topped grass. The calm loveliness of the village made her cry in protest at having to leave. Her eyes would light on some one thing or other and grow misty with tears. She had lost her love, her ungallant summer love. Others would come along. She had found a certain happiness that she would never loose again. Nothing now could ever spoil her inner peace, she thought.

Still, when Yves' Ford went by, Rosanne's heart often ached, especially on the last day of summer when she saw

Eve in the front seat on the way to Petit Lac. Yves turned his head away to escape her stare, and for a long time she kept her eyes on the slight cloud of dust that rose behind the car. A portion of her heart was going off with him. "When will it ever be completely free?" she wondered.

As if rooted to the sidewalk, she watched the speck the car had become. Finally it disappeared behind some trees. She was so absorbed that she did not hear a man's voice calling to her, *"Mam'selle. . . .* Hey, *Mam'selle,* come down to earth."

He was laughing, and so was the older man in the car with him. Both of them were looking at Rosanne with decided interest.

"You were far away . . ."

The young man was teasing her, and she couldn't help smiling back at him. She was learning to hide her thoughts.

"Are we on the right road to Petit Lac?" he asked. "They told us we could camp there tonight. Is it this way?"

"Yes, straight ahead." She pointed in the direction Yves and Eve had gone.

"Thanks, *chérie!*"

He pretended to lift a hat he wasn't wearing. He had blond curly hair, blue eyes and a clean-cut, intelligent face. She couldn't help liking him; his smile was so ingratiating.

"You wouldn't show us the way, no?" he asked, opening the door and getting out of his car. He towered above her. "I am André, and this is my father, Judge Saint-Germain. We are from Montréal. Ville-Marie is the last stop of our camping trip."

"Come on, André," said his father. "We're keeping this young lady."

The young man made a comically disappointed grimace, let out a sigh, and said, returning to his seat, "Too bad children must obey their parents."

He turned to Rosanne and pleaded, "At least, tell me your name, so that I can come back to Ville-Marie and find you again. You're sure you're real?"

Rosanne laughed, blithe as a lark, the way she used to laugh before she met Yves, with a merry, lively, cheery sound, her eyes brighter, her cheeks as rosy as her name, and she said, stooping a little to see his blue eyes under the car top, "We might meet again. I'm from Montréal, too."

"Please tell me your name."

"Rosanne."

"Rosanne . . . ?"

"Only Rosanne. You will have to find me with only that clue."

"I hope we meet again, Rosanne."

"I hope we do too, André," she said, and was sincere.

The car sped off in the dust along the same road Yves had taken. Later, much later, Rosanne would be driving off in that car. She was to spend her life with that blue-eyed man for whom her bittersweet summer had prepared her.

But that is another story.